PRAISE FOR BETTE LEE CROSBY'S NOVELS

A Million Little Lies

"Steeped in Secrets and Southern Charm, A Million Little Lies is both heartbreaking and heartwarming. A tale about forgiveness and family and what it means to finally find your true home."

— Barbara Davis, bestselling author of
The Last of the Moon Girls

"Heart-wrenching and heartwarming, a novel to satisfy your soul and leave your heart feeling happier."

— *Linda's Book Obsession*

"A quietly powerful story of relationships, trust, truth, lies, and the possibilities of forgiveness — an unforgettable ending."

— Patricia Sands, author of the bestselling
Love in Provence Series

Emily, Gone

"Heart-wrenching and heartwarming. A page turner until the end."

— Ashley Farley, bestselling author of *Only One Life*

"An extraordinary book that raises questions about love, family, faith, and forgiveness. This one will stay with me for quite some time."

— Camille DiMaio, bestselling author of
The Way of Beauty

"A beautiful story that will being you to tears! The writing is flawless! Definitely one of the most beautiful books I've read this year!"

— *Book Nerd*

A Year of Extraordinary Moments

"One of those rare books that makes you believe in the power of love. Filled with memorable characters and important life lessons, a Southern treat to the last page."

— Anita Hughes, author of *California Summer*

"Throughout this book, the author beautifully explores the theme of letting go of the past while preserving its best parts . . ."

— *Kirkus Reviews*

The Summer of New Beginnings

"This women's fiction novel is full of romance, the power of friendship and the bond of sisters."

— *The Charlotte Observer*

"A heartwarming story about family, forgiveness, and the magic of new beginnings."

— Christine Nolfi, bestselling author of *Sweet Lake*

"A heartwarming, captivating, and intriguing story about the importance of family ... The colorful cast of characters are flawed, quirky, mostly loyal, determined and mostly likable."

— *Linda's Book Obsession*

"Crosby's Southern voice comes through in all of her books and lends a believable element to everything she writes. *The Summer of New Beginnings* is no exception."

— *Book Chat*

Spare Change

"Skillfully written, *Spare Change* clearly demonstrates Crosby's ability to engage her readers' rapt attention from beginning to end. A thoroughly entertaining work of immense literary merit."

— *Midwest Book Review*

"Love, loss and unexpected gifts ... Told from multiple points of view, this tale seeped from the pages and wrapped itself around my heart."

— *Caffeinated Reviewer*

More than anything, *Spare Change* is a heartwarming book, which is simultaneously intriguing and just plain fun."

— *Seattle Post-Intelligencer*

Passing Through Perfect

"This is Southern fiction at its best: spiritually infused, warm, and family-oriented."

— *Midwest Book Reviews*

"Crosby's characters take on heartbreak and oppression with dignity, courage, and a shaken but still strong faith in a better tomorrow."

— IndieReader

The Twelfth Child

"Crosby's unique style of writing is timeless and her character building is inspirational."

— Layered Pages

"Crosby draws her characters with an emotional depth that compels the reader to care about their challenges, to root for their success, and to appreciate their bravery."

— Gayle Swift, author of ABC, Adoption & Me

"Crosby's talent lies in not only telling a good compelling story, but telling it from a unique perspective … Characters stay with you because they are simply too endearing to go away."

— Reader Views

Baby Girl

"Crosby weaves this story together in a manner that feels like a huge patchwork quilt. All the pieces and tears come together to make something beautiful."

— Michele Randall, Readers' Favorite

"Crosby is a true storyteller, delving into the emotions, relationships, and human dynamics—the cracks which break us, and ultimately make us stronger."

— J. D. Collins, Top 1000 reviewer

BLUEBERRY HILL

A Story of Sisters

ALSO BY BETTE LEE CROSBY

Magnolia Grove Series
The Summer of New Beginnings
A Year of Extraordinary Moments

The Wyattsville Series
Spare Change
Jubilee's Journey
Passing Through Perfect
The Regrets of Cyrus Dodd
Beyond the Carousel

The Memory House Series
Memory House
The Loft
What the Heart Remembers
Baby Girl
Silver Threads

Serendipity Series
The Twelfth Child
Previously Loved Treasures

Stand-Alone Titles
Emily Gone
Cracks in the Sidewalk
What Matters Most
Wishing for Wonderful
Blueberry Hill
Life in the Land of IS: The Amazing True Story of Lani Deauville

BLUEBERRY HILL

A Story of Sisters

BETTE LEE CROSBY

BENT PINE PUBLISHING

BENT PINE PUBLISHING
Port Saint Lucie, FL

Published in the United States of America

For Donna…

I love you and miss you still.

Sisters

My sister killed herself, and I will forever carry the weight of it being partly my fault. I didn't hand her a weapon, but I looked the other way.

I didn't just look the other way; I envied her lifestyle. If given the chance, I would have gladly become her: carefree, irresponsible, and living every moment to the fullest. Of course, back then we had no way of knowing what harm could come from a bit of fun. It was simply a few drinks and a cigarette.

I was the eldest of three sisters, and, according to Mama, responsible for any and all wrongdoing of my siblings. This rule applied regardless of my involvement or lack of involvement in the event. Whether the baby smeared crayon across the bedroom room wall or Donna came home carrying the smell of a skunk, Mama held me responsible.

"You're the oldest; you know better," she would say. "It's up to you to watch your sisters and make sure they stay out of trouble."

"But, Mama," I'd argue, "I wasn't even there!"

"Doesn't matter. You're the oldest and you're responsible."

CURTAILING ANYTHING DONNA DID was like trying to slow the winds of a hurricane. Even now as I look back and try to remember how it all began, I know I couldn't have done anything. Donna was who she was, and nothing would ever change her. She was a female version of Fonzi, the popular character from the 1970s show *Happy Days*. She was the popular girl, the cool girl, the one everybody tried to emulate. Looking at Donna in those teenage years, you could easily believe she was destined to live a golden life. But things don't always turn out the way we expect.

In that last year, I asked her, "If you could do it all over again, would you do anything differently?"

She shrugged. "Maybe."

That was about the closest I ever saw Donna come to having regrets.

IN THE EARLY DAYS

For as far back as I can remember, Donna would set her eye on something and go after it with such gusto that she couldn't possibly fail.

The earliest evidence of this came when she was seven and entered a Dairy Queen Contest. The prize was whatever the winner wanted—a sundae, a banana split, a blizzard, anything. She just had to put her name on the entry form and drop it in the box. The minute that slip of paper left Donna's hand she began planning what she'd choose when she won.

She dropped her entry in the box on Monday, then went back on Tuesday to check when the drawing would be held.

"Saturday," the kid behind the counter told her. "Not until Saturday morning."

For the whole week she counted off the days. Five

more days 'til Saturday…four more. Three more, until at last Saturday came.

At eight-thirty on Saturday morning, Donna was there, ready and waiting, but the Dairy Queen didn't open until ten o'clock. So she sat on the curb and waited. When they finally slid the service window open she hurried over.

"Is it time for the drawing yet?" she asked.

"Not yet, kid," the clerk answered. "About noon, that's when we do it."

Disappointed, but not defeated, she sat back down on the curb and continued to wait. That's when I came into the picture. Donna had been gone for several hours, and Mama sent me to search for her. Having accomplished my mission I plopped down on the curb beside her, and she told me the story.

"THE GUY AT THE window told me pretty soon," Donna says. "He promised pretty soon they're gonna pull the lucky name."

She smiles this big, wide, toothy grin and with all the confidence in the world tells me, "I'm gonna win. I know I'm gonna win. If you stay here, I'll share some of my banana split."

You hate to tell your kid sister she's nuttier than a fruitcake, but… She's the only kid there, nobody else in the entire parking lot, and she's been sitting there for more than three hours waiting to win this banana split.

"Mama told me to bring you home," I say.

"Not now!" she says with a gasp. "He's almost ready to announce the winner!"

I know spending another hour there is sure to get us both in trouble, but what the heck. I wait while she goes up to the window for what was probably the fourth or fifth time.

"Is it time yet, mister?" she asks.

"Yeah, it's time." With that the guy sticks his hand in this box and pulls out a piece of paper. Without showing it to anyone, he looks at her with wide-eyed pretense. "Holy cow, I can't believe this! What did you say your name was, kid?"

"Donna, Donna Sue Motley." My sister's face now shows an ear-to-ear smile.

"You're the winner," the guy says with a reasonably straight face. "Yeah, you're sure enough the winner."

"I'm the winner! I'm the winner!" Donna screams, jumping up and down. "I knew it, I just knew it."

"Okay, kid, you can have a banana split, a sundae, or anything else you want."

"I want a banana split," she says, "with two spoons."

"Here you are; two spoons."

The guy hands her the biggest banana split I have ever seen in all my life. We sit there on the curb and eat the whole thing. On the way home she says, "See, I told you I was gonna win."

LOOKING BACK, THE GROWNUP me knows it most likely wasn't her name on that piece of paper, but it doesn't matter. Donna got the prize because she had the tenacity and grit to believe.

Of course, this was one of those magical things that happened way back when I still believed her stretch of life would one day be paved with streets of gold.

Shortly after school started that fall, Mama got sick. For three days straight she remained in bed. Daddy made dinner all that week, and then on Friday afternoon he came home early and took her to the doctor. They came home smiling, so I had to assume there was nothing much wrong.

On Saturday afternoon Mama took Donna and me to the Sweet Shoppe for sodas, and we had what she called a woman-to-woman talk.

"DOCTOR LAVINE TOLD ME and your daddy that we're going to have a baby," Mama explains. "So until I get to feeling better, you girls will have to pitch in and help with the household chores."

Once that's out in the open, Mama spends the duration of her talk detailing the responsibilities of older sisters. Donna doesn't buy it, but I puff myself up with a sense of importance. The way Mama makes it sound, I'm practically going to be in charge of the newborn baby. (In retrospect, I believe it was the "in-charge" part that was the charmer.)

Donna is not of the same opinion.

"Can't you tell the doctor you don't want the baby?"

"Why would I do a thing like that?"

Donna scrunches her face and frowns.

Thinking Mama might give weight to such a thought and cause me to lose my newly-acquired level of responsibility, I jump in. "I think it's neat we're going to have a baby sister."

"Sister?" Donna echoes. "That's even worse. Tommy Barnes has a new baby sister, and she cries all the time."

"All babies cry," Mama says.

Given that fact Donna continues to argue in favor of no baby or at the very least have it be a boy. "Where's that baby gonna sleep?" she asks, then quickly adds, "Not in my room, I hope."

"I'm thinking you'll move over and share Bette's room; then I can put the baby in your room," Mama says.

"Oh, great," Donna grumbles.

The baby issue is not off to a great start as far as Donna is concerned, and she spends the next six months hoping it'll be a boy.

When the baby finally arrives the following February it's a girl. Donna is so disappointed she asks

Mama if she can get a dog because she didn't get a brother. Mama says no, she'll have to learn to live with a sister.

FOR SEVERAL MONTHS DONNA grumbled about the fact that I got a girl baby like I wanted and she couldn't even have a dog.

"If I can't have a dog," she said, "how about a cat?"

The answer was still no.

The following July Donna decided to do something about getting herself a pet. It was generally a sure sign of trouble when Donna took matters into her own hands.

WHEN I OPEN THE door I all but faint from the smell. There stands Donna with her friend, Alma. They have a skunk locked in a wooden crate. It's not one of those tame, de-skunked critters. No, this is the real thing. The two of them had gone into the woods, set a trap, and caught a skunk!

"Mama!" I scream. "You're not going to believe what Donna did!"

"Blabbermouth," Donna says with a scowl.

Mama gets a whiff of that skunk long before she reaches the door. Standing at the far end of the kitchen, she hollers for me to have both kids strip down to their bare skin out there on the porch. "Then take their clothes down to the incinerator," she adds.

"Not me," I say, "I'm not touching that stuff."

"You've got two seconds to get going," Mama says and waggles a finger in the direction of the garbage room.

Mama puts both kids into a hot tub of soapy water and scrubs until their skin turns red. She does it a half dozen times, but when we go to bed that night Donna still stinks.

"Don't you know skunks can't be pets?" I ask.

Donna is still mad at this point, so she rolls over, faces the wall, and doesn't bother to answer.

THE YEAR I TURNED thirteen I made two very important discoveries. I learned that I had no athletic ability whatsoever, but I also figure out I was blessed with a fair bit of business sense. Both of these revelations surfaced the day Donna showed me how to ride a two-wheel bike.

A NUMBER OF SMALL New Jersey towns are tucked behind the cities. They're places few people have heard of and fewer still have visited. Ridgefield was just such a place. Most kids rode their bike to school. I say most kids because there was a handful of misfits who, like me, didn't.

Patty was one too. Walking to school meant walking uphill, and Patty didn't do uphill. She couldn't. She was so overweight I doubt there was a bicycle with a sturdy enough seat. Her mother drove her to school. I walked.

Walking to school was bad enough, but walking home was more often than not a humiliating event. I usually ended up walking alongside Patty. We were in the same class and we traveled in the same direction; it was unavoidable. Once I lingered behind thinking she'd be long gone when I left, but she was there, waiting.

"What happened?" she asked. "Mister Lorenzo keep you after class?"

"I was cleaning out my locker," I lied.

Even though the walk home was downhill, Patty huffed and puffed like a dying steam engine. I should have helped her. I should have offered to carry her books or stopped long enough for her to catch her breath. But I didn't.

I was at the age where everyone's opinion counted and when kids laughingly called out names like Fatty Patty. I cringed. I was afraid that through the factor of association I would forever be linked to the fat girl, the outcast. Now I look back and think how shallow such thoughts were, but when you're a shy teenage girl a breeze is seen as a windstorm. Everything is a threat to your fragile image.

AFTER MONTHS OF WALKING home alongside Patty, I finally break down and ask Donna to teach me how to ride a two-wheel bike. I sit on the stoop in front of our house watching her circle past me on the walkway like the bareback queen in a circus act, and all the while I'm thinking I am never going to be able to do this.

"It's easy," Donna yells. She pulls back on the handlebars, does another whirly, then lets go and still doesn't fall. The truth is I wish she would—not hard enough to actually break something, just hard enough to injure her ego.

It's a sibling rivalry thing. All kids have it. You might not always see it but it's there, mixed in with brotherly or sisterly love. It shows its ugly face in the ordinary moments of life, but when hearts are broken or lives shattered it inevitably gives way to love.

"Come on! I'll show you how if you do that report for me!"

Grudgingly, I say I'll do her book report if she'll teach me how to ride the bike. She agrees.

I climb on the bike and get seated. The oval courtyard now looks like the Indianapolis Speedway. Donna says not to worry, she's going to steady the bike and run beside me as I circle the walkway.

"Maybe we'd better start with something smaller."

"Smaller?" She gives me a look. "Start pedaling."

I do, and she runs beside me steadying the bike. Unfortunately, the second she lets go the front wheel wobbles and I topple over. I wasn't going very fast so there wasn't far to fall. Nothing but my pride is injured. We repeat the process over and over, but I can't move past my fear of failure.

Two hours and a dozen falls later, we take a break and flop down on the grass mogul beside the mailboxes. The two-story brick buildings circling the courtyard line up like Monopoly houses. Each of these buildings has a front porch littered with tricycles, pedal cars, and other toys. I know a lot of these kids because I babysit for them on Friday or Saturday nights when their parents go to the movies or an Elks Club dance. The families trust me because I don't bring boyfriends over like some of the high school girls. Besides, they know my mother is nearby and keeps an eye on me.

As I sit there rubbing my shin, Missus Keller sticks her head out the door and warns her redheaded toddler, "Don't you dare take a step off this porch, Bobby."

The kid defiantly starts down the steps, and the mother yells again.

"Get back up here! One more step, and you're in trouble!"

Bobby looks back at his mama then scrambles down the other three steps and takes off running across the courtyard. Seconds later poor Missus Keller starts chasing after Bobby; she's got his baby sister tucked under her arm.

By now the baby is screaming and the two-year-old terror is staying just out of reach, laughing like it's a big joke. Without realizing it, he runs toward me. I nab him and hold him until his mother gets there.

In between yelling at Bobby and jiggling the crying baby, Mrs. Keller hands me two quarters and says, "Thanks, Bette. I wish I had someone like you to keep an eye on him every morning so I could get my housework done in peace."

I can't believe my ears. "You mean you'd pay a babysitter to watch him even if you're at home?"

"Um-hmm. The only problem is I can't spare more than five dollars a week. I doubt a sitter would take a job for such poor pay." With that, she trots back across the courtyard, both kids in tow.

I turn to Donna. "Did you hear that?"

"Yeah, so?"

"So?" I repeat. Now I am on the knowing end of the conversation. "If I could make five bucks for every kid in this development, I'd be rich." I start counting the number of porches with kid toys.

"You'll be babysitting all summer. You won't have any time for fun." Donna scrunches her face into a look of disdain. "That's nuts."

"But if I watch them all together, at one time..." Now the wheels have started turning.

"At one time?" Donna says. "How?"

"I can have the mothers bring them to the kiddie playground every morning at nine o'clock and come pick them up at noon. We could organize games and let them play with each other –"

"Whaddaya mean 'we'?" Donna says. "I'm not babysitting those mean kids." She shakes her head side to side. "No way."

"You'd be a partner. Make a lot of money."

"Unh-unh!"

"It would only be three hours a day."

"Weekends?"

"No weekends," I promise.

"How much money?"

"Depends on how many kids we get." I start doing the math in my head. "We could charge five dollars for the whole week. That way it'd be so cheap all the moms will want their kids to come. I'll bet we could get at least twenty kids. That's one hundred dollars."

"I get half?"

"Of course not," I say, knowing I've got the upper hand for once. "It's my idea, and besides, I'll have all the business responsibility." A look of doubt starts creeping across her face so I quickly add, "But you'll get two dollars for every kid we watch. That's forty dollars a week."

Now she's interested. "Forty dollars? No working in the afternoon?"

"Yeah, providing we get twenty kids."

THAT JULY WE STARTED our baby-sitting business with more than forty kids, and I was raking in a whopping two hundred bucks a week. I saved most of my windfall. Of course I did; that's the kind of person I am. Part of that money went into a college fund, and the rest was set aside to buy new clothes for school.

Donna treated her friends to ice cream sodas, movies, and even a day at Palisades Amusement Park. Come September, she didn't have a dime left.

What can I say, we were different people.

Sometimes I wish I had been a little more like Donna. She did what she wanted to without caring about who liked it and who didn't. Not me. I worried about everything, including the possibility of becoming a social reject because I was still walking home with Fatty Patty.

A Time of Rebellion

I was fifteen when I discovered the next best thing to being Donna was having her for a sister. Granted, we were an unseemly pair, her in blue jeans and leather jacket, me in head-to-toe pink. Standing next to Donna, my narrow shoulders and small stature ran a poor second to her tall athletic build. With almost two years difference in our ages, I had the advantage of being older; she had the advantage of being bigger. This resulted in a long-standing argument as to who was the "big sister."

I can't begin to count the number of times I wished to be Donna. From time to time I would dress in her clothes and sashay across the room, looking to the mirror for validation. There was none. I could no more pretend to be my sister than she could pretend to be me. In time, I came to accept that I was what I was: a little girl with a fragile self-image. I was the wisher, the dreamer. Donna was the doer. I doubt she ever wished to be me. Perhaps in those last months she did, but it's not likely.

I AM NOT A PERSON who resorts to fisticuffs. Never. Under no circumstances. Not only do I lack the physical prowess to win such a battle, but a lifetime of hearing Mama say "A lady never fights. It's undignified and unacceptable" has taken root in my head.

In the heat of anger I let go of words: a snide comment or verbal put-down perhaps. But that's the extent of it. More often than not, I simply turn and walk away. Mama's countless admonitions about what she termed brawling did not have the same effect on Donna. She had no such inhibitions. I came to appreciate that the day I saw Sally Walther standing outside the drugstore.

IT STARTED BECAUSE OF Tommy Ballinger, a boy whose locker is two down from mine. Boys like Tommy rarely ask girls like me on dates, so when he does I get all giggly and jump at the chance.

Stupid move. I know Tommy has a thing with Sally, but when I glance over her picture is no longer stuck to his locker door.

"What's up with Sally?" I ask.

"She's history," Tommy tells me, and I believe it because it's what I want to believe.

On Friday night we go to the movies and out for sodas. Half the town sees us together at the Sweet Shoppe. I'm practically floating on a cloud and starting to picture myself wearing his varsity jacket.

This lasts for less than a day, because the next morning Sally spots me through the glass window of the drugstore and slams her fist against the palm of her other hand to illustrate what she has in mind.

Sally Walther is not a person willing to listen to words. I panic and telephone home. I plan on asking Mama to come and get me, but Donna answers.

"Mama's not home."

"Oh, crap." I sigh and explain my predicament. "I'll wait here. When Mama gets home tell her—" I hear a click.

"Donna?"

Nothing. It's obvious she's hung up the phone, so I call back. This time there is no answer.

I stay in the phone booth where I am safe. From here I can keep an eye on Sally and her two cronies. I watch her make a few more threatening gestures, and I try to come up with another plan.

Three times I try calling home; still no answer. As I dial again, four kids on bicycles round the corner. It's Donna and her friends.

I'm expecting the worst, but when Donna comes to

a stop and drops her bike on the sidewalk Sally makes no move.

Donna sashays over, pokes a finger toward Sally's chest, and starts saying something. I can't hear the words, but the sight of it gives me courage. I venture out of the phone booth and head for the door. As I step outside Sally starts to walk away. She turns, gives me a disgusted look, then keeps walking.

"What'd you say to her?" I ask.

Donna shrugs. "I said she oughta leave you alone."

"Or what?"

Donna never tells me what she said, but weeks later I hear that she'd threatened to hold Sally down and shave her head bald. By then the trouble has died down, and Sally's picture is again hanging in Tommy Ballinger's locker.

YOU'LL NOTICE WHEN I speak of Donna's movement I use the word "sashay" not "walk." That's because walking is different. Walking moves a body by simply placing one foot in front of the other. Sashaying takes attitude, the sort of attitude Donna had. It takes command of a room and draws people in like a magnet. It says, *Here I am, and this is what I am! If you don't like it, well, that's just too bad!* Only a fearless person can sashay into a room. Only a person like my sister.

Having such an attitude is both a gift and a curse. It gives the bravado to muscle through life but adds in the type of recklessness that can one day rob you of all you are.

THREE YEARS LATER, BEFORE she finishes high school, Donna runs away from home. No note, no goodbye, no nothing. She just up and disappears one morning after she and Mama have yet another argument.

It starts when Donna gets ready for school. Mama takes a look at how she's dressed and says, "You're not leaving here with those blue jeans on!"

"Yes, I am," Donna says and heads for the door.

Mama, who is a snip shorter than me, steps in front of the door with her arms folded. "No, you're not! Wearing blue jeans to school is unacceptable."

"Everybody wears them." Donna tries to squeeze by Mama first on one side and then the other.

Mama stays with it. Whichever way Donna moves, Mama moves. The truth is that Donna outsizes Mama by nearly ten inches, and she is all muscle. If she'd a mind to, she could pick Mama up and set her aside. But that's something not even Donna will do.

Anyway, the argument rages on. Just words, no pushing or shoving, but the words are loud and repetitive.

"You know what people call a girl who dresses like

that?" Before Donna can squeeze in a word, Mama answers her own question. "Trash, they say. That girl's nothing but trash!"

"You think I care what people say?"

"Well, I care! I don't want any daughter of mine—"

"Enough!" Daddy finally yells. After twenty minutes of them going at it, he is sick to death of listening.

"Donna Sue," he thunders. "Get back to your room, and if you come out wearing those jeans again you won't be going anywhere."

When Daddy calls any of us kids by our full name, it means we're in big trouble. Donna turns on her heel and heads back to her room. It's a good fifteen minutes before she comes out again. When she does she's wearing a pleated skirt.

"Ah, now." Mama gives a sigh of satisfaction. "That looks much better."

I can't recall Donna answering, but if she did it was nothing more than a grunt. Then she walks out the door.

Mama believes that for once she's won a battle with Donna, but I'm wary that such a victory came too easily. I'm right.

That afternoon Mama finds the skirt and Donna's schoolbooks on the back porch. She comes in waving that skirt in the air and fussing to beat the band.

"This is the last straw!" she hollers. "When that smart aleck gets home from school, we'll see about this!"

I'm the only one within hearing range but that doesn't stop Mama from fussing. The whole of that afternoon she argues with Donna, who is nowhere to be seen. Donna doesn't come home for supper, and she still isn't home when I fall into bed at eleven-thirty.

Given Donna's rebellious nature, it isn't anything for her to thumb her nose at curfew and come home whenever she's good and ready. So at first nobody worries about it.

Mama might be a bit worried, but her concern is hidden beneath a thick layer of mad. She sits in the living room chair and waits for Donna all night long. When morning arrives and Donna still isn't home, Mama starts calling around.

First it's her friends. Then the teachers. When everybody claims they haven't seen Donna since day before yesterday, Mama calls the hospital and police station. That same morning, a patrol car arrives and sits in our driveway for a good three hours. The officer helps Mama fill out a missing person report, and when he asks what Donna was wearing when she left home Mama has to admit it's probably the blue jeans. Before noon, the police department sends out an all points bulletin and starts checking the local haunts.

After a few days of searching it becomes obvious that Donna is gone. She continues to be listed as a missing person, but it's a file now relegated to the far corner of a junior detective's desk.

"Most likely a runaway," the detective says. "Runaway kids seldom leave a trail."

Hearing such news, Mama falls to pieces and keeps imagining Donna lying dead in some God-forsaken ditch. Mixed in with all her worry is a fear that she's the one responsible.

"It's my fault," Mama moans. "I should have just let her wear whatever she wanted to wear."

Daddy tries to calm her down by rubbing her back and saying things like she was only doing what any mother would have done. But Mama will have none of it. She swears that Donna's disappearance is the Lord's way of punishing her for being a terrible mother.

A week later Daddy takes Mama to the doctor, and they come home with enough tranquilizers to put a horse to sleep. "If your mama doesn't get some rest," Daddy says, "she's going to have a nervous breakdown."

By that time the baby, who Mama had named Geri after herself, is five years old. While she doesn't need diapering and feeding, she does need to be watched over and that becomes my job.

It's the start of a very long six months.

THE PRODIGAL DAUGHTER

In time the Portsmouth, Virginia, police found Donna and sent her home. By then a full six months had rolled by and Mama was little more than a shell of her former self.

On the morning she left home, Donna had hitchhiked to Route 95 then caught a ride with a black family headed south. She didn't know their names, where they came from, or where they were headed. She only knew they were willing to give her a ride and share the sandwiches they carried in a cooler.

Donna left home thinking she'd find a place to stay at our aunt's house in Portsmouth, but before long she realized Mama would be the first one Aunt Ida called. Not good.

I wish I could tell you how my sister survived those first few days, but she never told us and we had no way of finding out. What we do know is that when

25

the police located her, she was working at a barbeque stand and living in a furnished room she'd rented herself.

Anyone with a brain in their head would wonder why an employer would hire a girl who was barely sixteen, but Donna was tall, wide-shouldered, and brassy. Add that to her sashay and you couldn't tell whether she was sixteen or thirty, so no one bothered to ask questions.

Donna returned home a different person. Before she left she would sneak an occasional cigarette, but now she smoked one after another and was openly defiant about it. Mama, who had gone through months and months of torture worrying about her middle child lying dead in a ditch, no longer argued. When Donna lit up Mama pinched her eyebrows together, then turned and looked the other way.

Without saying a single word, Donna had won the longstanding battle.

THAT SIX-MONTH HOLE IN our lives didn't just change Donna; it changed us all. Before she ran off, we were a regular family with everyday differences of opinion and arguments. From time to time we might have exchanged a few sassy words or banged a door, but that was it. The next day we'd go about our business like nothing ever happened. Once Donna went missing, we became a house of sorrow. It was as if her body was in the living room cold as ice, and Mama wasn't sure whether or not to bury her.

I thought after Donna came home we'd go back to being the way we were, but I was wrong. We just moved from being a family of sorrow to one of fear. It felt like there was a bomb strapped to each of us, and one wrong word would set off an explosion.

We didn't argue about anything. You might think that's good, but it's not. When some people stop arguing, it means they've stopped caring. I don't think we'd stopped caring. We were just too fearful to show it. Especially Mama.

From that time forward Mama was a smaller person, and she had little to say. More than anyone else Mama was afraid of those bombs. Anything from a harsh whisper to the bong of the doorbell could jangle her nerves and cause her to need another gulp of what she called her nerve medicine.

In truth it was rye whiskey she'd poured into a small plastic bottle. That bottle went everywhere Mama went, and if she left the house she carried it in her handbag. Sometimes when I leaned in to kiss her goodnight I caught the smell of whiskey on her breath.

Before the hole in our lives the only time I ever saw Mama take a drink was at a party, and then it was mixed with a tall glass of Coca Cola.

Daddy liked to drink on a regular basis, but Mama didn't. When she pulled out the bottle and took a swallow, she scrunched up her face and drank it like medicine. I would have felt a lot better about her drinking whiskey if she'd enjoyed it the way Daddy did.

ONCE SHE CAME BACK home, Donna didn't give school a second thought. Several times Daddy mentioned it but Mama, afraid Donna would run off again, just hushed him.

"Now, Sam," Mama would say, "don't go picking at Donna. She'll go back to school when she's ready to."

Even a fool could see Donna wouldn't ever go back to school. Mama saw it, but she didn't want to risk losing her daughter over it. So that's the way it went. When Mama or Daddy set a curfew time it whizzed right by Donna, and while she didn't argue about it she didn't abide by it either. For Donna there were no more rules. It was as if she'd crossed into adulthood when she'd crossed the state line.

TWO WEEKS AFTER SHE was sent home, Donna went out and got herself another job. This time it was working as a roller skating carhop at the root beer stand on Route 17. She wore what she called a uniform: white shorts and an orange tee shirt. The tee shirt was plenty snug, but the shorts were so skimpy they could easy as not be mistaken for underpants. Mama disapproved of both the job and the uniform, but she never said a word about either one.

The root beer stand was a half-hour drive from our house and when Donna first got the job she was three months shy of being old enough for a driver's license, so Mama took her to work every day.

"You want me to pick you up at eleven?" Mama would ask.

Donna would shake her head. "I'll catch a ride with friends," she'd say without ever specifying who those friends were.

Whoever they were they obviously didn't have a mama breathing down their neck, because Donna didn't usually come in until three or four in the morning.

By fall Donna had enough money to buy a car; not a brand new one but way better than what I drove. Back then she lived a life most young girls wouldn't dare to dream of. She had money, a great car, a lineup of guys wanting to date her, and more friends than you could count.

But the problem with flying through life at such a breakneck speed is you forget that sooner or later you'll need to slam on the brakes.

Less than six months after she got that car, Donna moved out of Mama and Daddy's house and into an apartment she shared with four other girls. It wasn't even a real apartment. It was the basement of an old house in Lodi where the owner had put up enough wallboard for two bedrooms and a kitchen. It didn't matter that they had to go through the furnace room to get to where they slept, Donna had her freedom and that's what she wanted.

Mama cried for days after Donna left. "Living like that, she'll get her fool self killed," Mama said sobbing. Although she had no way of knowing it at the time, she wasn't all that far from the truth.

I DON'T SUPPOSE ANYONE will ever know what really happened in Virginia, but it changed Donna. She was gone six months, but she came home with years of learning. She hadn't just survived she'd thrived and was ready to take on the world. Her new friends were people who thought as she thought. Like her, they were looking for a good time. They were older than her, but with Donna you couldn't tell if she was sixteen or thirty-six. So their way of life became hers. She matched them drink for drink and smoke for smoke.

Guy with a Guitar

It's one thing to be fearless and yet another to throw caution to the wind, which is what Donna did the night she met Charlie. The next morning she woke with stars in her eyes.

"He's in a band, and he's the lead singer," she told me. She went on about how he'd eyed her throughout the evening and slipped her a note saying where he'd be playing the next night.

"LET'S GO," SHE SAYS. "It'll be a blast!"

Although I'm not by nature a club person, I have to admit Donna's excitement reels me in. "Okay."

That night we get dressed up and leave the house at ten-thirty.

"This is kind of late to be going out, isn't it?" I say.

"Late?" Donna gives me a sideways look of disbelief. "You look desperate if you get there before eleven."

"Oh, okay."

The club we go to is in Brooklyn. It's little more than a hole in the wall, a narrow brick building with three steps leading down and loud music coming up.

"This is the place?" I ask. Already I'm thinking this is a bad idea.

She nods. "Cool, huh?"

I follow her inside and stay close behind. This is a place where I feel neither comfortable nor safe, but Donna loves it so I try to love it with her.

We stand off to the side and order drinks. For a while we listen to the music; then when the band takes a break this short guy with an oversized nose starts walking toward us.

Donna pokes an elbow in my rib. "This is the guy," she whispers.

At first I think she's kidding, but she's not.

"Hey, Charlie," she says.

He sticks his arm out, flattens his hand against the wall, and leans into Donna. "I figured you'd be here."

I'm amazed that this is the guy my beautiful, cool, with-it sister is crazy about. I don't get it, but she obviously likes him so I say nothing.

Before he heads back to the bandstand, Charlie says, "When we close up, we're getting together at Mike's. You want to come?"

I say no. Donna says yes, and she's driving.

We don't get home until five o'clock that morning. I am weary to the bone, but Donna is the happiest I've ever seen her.

Now I look back and wonder: if I had refused to go, would she have gone anyway? If she hadn't gone, would they still have connected in some other time and place? There is great wisdom in hindsight, but even hindsight has its blind spots. And this, I suppose, is one of them.

AS IT TURNED OUT, Charlie was not the party boy Donna described. He was a brutish man with a callous way of thinking and a nose that overshadowed his face.

"Be careful," I told my sister, "he reeks of trouble."

"Careful is for people who are afraid of life," she answered.

Five months later Donna was pregnant and they got married. They didn't have a white-gown, invite-all-your-friends ceremony but a courthouse quickie. For Donna that was enough. Beneath the crusty exterior beat the heart of a wild woman ready to settle down.

Having a baby, that's what changed her. The baby, and the fact that she'd actually fallen in love with a man who loved himself far more than he loved her.

Seven months after the wedding, their son was born. She named the boy after his daddy, but within the year she and Charlie got divorced. He'd left her for a new groupie who followed the band from place to place. A younger groupie. One who didn't come with a baby attached.

Donna never cried. Not once. You could almost see through the hole in her heart, but she covered it with a breastplate of resolution.

Instead of giving way to the hurt, she moved in with Mama and Daddy and resumed her roller-skating carhop job. She also went back to late-night drinking and smoking. But there was one change: she now pulled herself out of bed every morning and took care of the baby.

You might expect that she'd be a terrible mother, but you'd be wrong. Donna was not exactly orthodox in her manner of handling things. There was no set schedule, no dinner on the table at the dot of six, no eight o'clock bedtime. But she held little Charlie so close to her heart it was as if they were one person.

A YEAR LATER DONNA told me she was getting back together with Charlie and they were planning to be remarried.

I gasped. "You're kidding! Why would you do that? He's a terrible father, he lies, cheats—" I caught myself mid-sentence and stopped.

Donna eyed me with a puzzled look. A look that questioned why I'd say such a thing. She didn't even answer.

"I'm sorry if I've spoken out of turn," I said, "but you're so special. You deserve so much more. Is this really what you want?"

I stopped talking when I noticed Donna nervously tapping her fingers on the table and fingering the pack of cigarettes in front of her.

A long minute passed before she shook one loose, lit it, and pulled a long slow drag.

"Yes, it's what I want," she answered. "I really love Charlie."

That was the end of the discussion.

The Madness of Marriage

Seven months after the second courthouse marriage, Donna gave birth to a daughter. By then she'd given up her roller skating carhop job.

Charlie's mother, who at one time praised her son for being what she called an entertainer, now looked down on his pastime with disdain.

"You're a married man with two babies!" she said. "It's time to settle down."

She withdrew a considerable amount of money from her savings account, bought a house two blocks from where she lived, and then handed the keys to Charlie.

"I'm not expecting rent," she said, "but I am expecting you to give up that trashy job!"

Charlie did. For a while. He took a day job and began work as an assistant administrator in a local college.

At first it was good. Caring for the two babies brought out a softness I'd never before seen in Donna. Charlie, not so much. He grew restless, itchy to do something more than hurry home to a pot roast dinner and watch television.

"Why don't you take the kids to the playground?" Donna would ask, but his only answer would be a look of incredulity.

AFTER A FEW YEARS of working a day job Charlie pulled his guitar from the closet and began plucking at the strings again. At first it was a casual thing, but in time he went back to joining the group.

"Tony's got a broken arm," he told Donna. "They need a fill-in."

"For how long?" she asked suspiciously.

"A week, maybe two."

A week turned into a month and a month into several more, and when Donna reminded him of his promise to leave the band Charlie fell back on the pretense of needing money.

"The car needs a new radiator," he said. After that it was the back fence that would need to be replaced and an extraordinarily high heating bill. When he piled the financial needs on top of one another, Donna volunteered to get a job and she did.

No longer interested in being a roller skating carhop, she began to search the newspapers for a job close to the house so she'd be there when the kids needed her.

One morning as we sat with steamy cups of coffee and searched the want ads, a smile lit up her face. "Here's a great one," she said. "Bank teller."

Bear in mind that Donna was a high school dropout. While others her age finished high school and moved on to college, she was skating from car to car with overloaded trays of root beer.

I GLANCE AT THE AD then look back at my sister. "This says college graduate. No experience required."

Donna laughs. "Well, I don't have any experience!"

"You also don't have any college," I remind her.

"That's probably something they're flexible on," she says. "Anyway, this job is perfect for me. It's close by; I can get the kids off to school and be home an hour after they are."

"I suppose it wouldn't hurt to try," I say, "but I wouldn't get my hopes up because of the college thing."

"Wonder what I should wear?" Donna muses. The next day she calls me, and I can practically see her smiling over the phone.

"I got it," she says.

"You did?" My surprise is obvious. "How'd you get around the college requirement?"

"I told them I went to school in California, but the building burned down and the records were lost."

"You're kidding," I exclaim.

She assures me she's not. "I was kind of nervous when they asked me the name of the college."

"What did you say?"

"Well, I remembered there was a college near where Aunt Jean used to live, and it really did burn down."

"That was nine years ago."

"Yeah, I know. I said when I went there it was called Chico College, but since then they've changed the name and I'm not too sure of what the new name is."

"You told them that and still got the job?"

"Yep," she answers proudly.

I rest my case. Donna was an enigma. She was that rare person you couldn't help but like. She was still the kid who had enough grit and determination to win a banana split, only this time it was a job.

SHE STAYED AT THE bank for almost ten years, advanced to become the branch manager, and was written about in the local newspaper for nailing a fraudulent check casher. Without him being any the wiser, she pushed the silent alarm and then stalled and kept him waiting long enough for the police to arrive.

The sad thing is that while Donna built a life for

their family, Charlie rebuilt a life of his own. A life based on wide-eyed groupies following him from place to place and serving up free sex.

More than once Donna suspected as much, but there's a long stretch between suspecting and knowing. It wasn't until Cyndi Lou happened along that she was forced into knowing. That was six months after Charlie went from playing once or twice a week to every night.

I'm certain the Cyndi Lou thing had been going on for quite a while, but it didn't surface until the Tuesday night Donna and I took the kids bowling.

WHILE I'M STILL PULLING on my shoes, Donna spots three of the fellows in Charlie's band in the lane next to us.

"Hey, Tony." She waves. "Aren't you guys playing tonight?"

This is a deer-in-the-headlights moment. The panic-stricken Tony looks down at his watch and says, "Holy shit, I lost track of the time." Then he and the other two hightail it out of there without bothering to finish the game.

"Son of a bitch," my sister says angrily. "He's at it again."

Her daughter, Debi, who is now thirteen going on thirty, says, "Don't be mad, Mom. Maybe there's a reason."

"I'm sure there's a reason," Donna answers. There's a hard crust on her words, but she leaves it at that and we go back to bowling. Donna laughs and talks as if nothing is wrong, but I can see inside my sister. I can see the heartbreak pushing against her skin.

DONNA SAYS NOTHING MORE about the incident until the next morning. Charlie sits at the table nursing a cup of coffee and she asks, "How was the gig last night?"

"Not bad," Charlie mumbles.

"Where'd you play?"

"A club in Brooklyn; you've never been there."

"You got in really late," Donna says casually. "Was it a long drive or a late set?"

"Both."

"Did Tony ride with you?"

"Yeah, him and Buck."

Donna nods, but she is already thinking of what she will do.

That afternoon she calls me and relates the story.

"Charlie's screwing around again," she says. Then she explains how she needs me to come with her. "He's playing at Club Fresco tonight, but I want to see where he goes after that."

Sensing trouble, I ask, "Are you sure this is what you want to do? Why don't you just confront Charlie with what you know and see what he has to say?"

She heaves a sigh that carries years of weariness. "I

already know what he'll say," she answers and gives no further explanation.

PART OF BEING A sister is sticking together in good times and bad. I don't have a good feeling about this, but I agree to go along. I almost know what will happen, but I also know that like all the times before Donna will forgive him. She will swallow her own hurt to keep her family together. Little Charlie is now fifteen and Debi is thirteen, but they are still her babies and she is fierce as a mama lion when it comes to protecting them. I guess she feels that having a cheating daddy is better than having none at all.

It's after ten when we drive to Club Fresco. She doesn't park in the street, nor does she park in the club parking lot. She parks alongside a delivery van left overnight in the lot beside the hardware store. She's already spotted Charlie's car, and from here she can keep an eye on it.

We sit there until shortly after one o'clock. Then handfuls of people start drifting out. It is a good half hour before we see Cyndi Lou come toddling through the door with Charlie. He walks her to her car, and before she climbs in he bends her over the front fender and kisses her with such ferocity that I feel embarrassed watching. I cannot fathom what is going through my sister's mind, but her face is a mask of stone.

"Maybe he's drunk," I suggest.

Donna shakes her head and says nothing.

After several minutes and a considerable amount of groping, Cyndi Lou climbs into her car and drives away.

"It's probably a just groupie thing," I say. "You know how these girls throw themselves at the singers."

"We'll see," Donna answers.

Charlie goes back into the club, and we continue to sit and watch his car. Fifteen minutes later he comes out, gets into his car, and drives away. Donna pulls out and follows him several car lengths back. We drive for almost twenty minutes; then he turns down a side street. Donna stops at the corner and watches. It is now two-fifteen, and there is only one house on this entire block with the porch light still lit. Charlie slows his little sports car and pulls into the driveway. Before he can unfold himself from the seat, Cyndi Lou is standing on the front step wearing panties and a lacy camisole. He climbs from the car, walks toward her, and again they embrace. His hands are all over her ass. They step inside and close the door.

"Son of a bitch," Donna says.

For several minutes, she sits there without speaking. Then she turns to me and says, "Brace yourself." She pulls out, guns the motor, and goes roaring down the street. I have no idea what she is planning, but she does. Just before we reach Cyndi Lou's house Donna swings the car to the other side of the street, thumps over the curb and part of a lawn, then makes a fast right and ploughs into the driveway, ramming Charlie's car from behind. The sports car crumples and smashes through the wooden garage door.

As Donna backs out of the driveway, Charlie comes running out in his underwear. Cyndi Lou follows him, pulling a robe over her nakedness.

"Crazy bitch!" Charlie yells.

Donna gives him the finger and drives off. His car is demolished, but the only damage to the fifteen-year-old tank she drives is a broken headlight.

THAT WAS THE END of their second marriage. Donna told Charlie she'd take the kids and he could have the house. And that's what happened.

I questioned such a move. "Don't you think you should tell him to get out and keep the house?"

"Nope," Donna answered. "It's his house. His mama bought it for him and he's entitled to keep it."

"But..."

"Forget it, Bette. I'm done with Charlie, his house, and his mama."

"But legally..."

"I don't care about legally," she said. "I wanted a daddy for my kids. Charlie's never really been one, and he's sure as hell not gonna be one now!"

That was the end of the conversation, and Donna never went back on what she'd decided. She took both kids, and they all squeezed themselves into a garden apartment that would've been cramped for one. They didn't have much in the way of material things, but they surely had a lot of love.

As the Years Passed

From time to time I hear someone talk about a person who doesn't have their priorities straight. That wasn't the case with Donna. Oh, it's true enough that she made some bad choices, but when it came to priorities, she knew exactly what hers were: the kids.

Donna was not a by-the-book mom. Things like schedules, curfews, and discipline had nothing to do with the way she raised the children. She was more of a friend than a parent. When I look back at these years, I picture my sister with seven or eight kids squeezed into her Volkswagen Bug; their heads hanging out the windows and poking up from the open sunroof as she drove through town beeping the horn to celebrate a football game win. The truth is Donna was the biggest kid of all.

I think those years, when she still had the children with her, were the happiest of Donna's life. Nobody can know for sure because while she was quick to share good times and fun, Donna never shared her heartache. Not even with me.

Sometimes I caught a glimpse of it. Times when Charlie's name came up or when she heard a song he sang. Times like that she'd light up another cigarette and move on without ever acknowledging the empty hole he'd left behind. The sad truth is that despite how little he had to give, Donna loved Charlie. An even sadder truth is that she kept on loving him for as long as she lived.

DONNA REMAINED IN NEW Jersey until the kids were out of school and on their own. Then she moved to Baltimore. Outside of Mama she didn't know a soul in Baltimore, but that didn't stop her.

"What's in Baltimore?" I asked.

Donna laughed. "Mama," she answered and that was all she said. There was no further explanation.

By that time our baby sister Geri and I were both married and pretty well ensconced in living our own lives.

The thing about being married is that you don't love your sister one pinprick less, but your days are wrapped up in the million things you have to do: work, laundry, cleaning, cooking, and the mile-long list of errands to run. Looking back I wish I'd have said *To hell with the laundry* and gone out with Donna every Saturday. I didn't see it that way then; I always thought there'd be another week, another Saturday, another time when we could get together and have fun. Having a sister is like having a thumb; you simply believe it will always be there, because how could you possibly get along without it?

Geri and I were doing fine, but Mama needed a friend. After Daddy died, she married a man with a hearing impairment and now spent most of her time hollering out questions or pointing to what she was talking about.

"Lord God," she told Donna, "you've got to come down here and keep me company, or I'll go stark raving mad!"

In a twist of fate few could predict, the child who caused Mama's nervous breakdown was the one who came to her rescue. Donna found an even smaller garden apartment two blocks from Mama's house, then packed up the handful of things she owned and moved.

MAMA AND DONNA HAD a number of good years together, years when they were more like girlfriends than mother and daughter. Now that Donna had acquired banking experience, getting a job was no problem. She'd go to work during the day, and when the bank closed at three o'clock she'd drive by, pick Mama up, and off they'd go.

When I picture Mama and Donna driving off together, Donna's always got a cigarette in her hand. I picture it that way because that's how it was.

"Those things are gonna be the death of you," Mama would complain.

Donna didn't care; she'd just laugh it off. "Everybody's gotta die sometime," she'd say and fire up another cigarette.

FEW PEOPLE KNEW DONNA as I did. We were close in age and grew up together. We shared a room and shared secrets no one else was privy to. Although we were as different as night and day, we were stuck together with the crazy glue of sisterhood. That's how it was and how it would always be. I saw the inside part of my sister that no one else could see.

In Baltimore Donna thrived, or at least she gave the appearance of thriving. She opened up with a personality that drew people in and made them want to be the one standing next to her. If she walked into a bar filled with strangers, she had nine new friends before she left.

Once she no longer had the responsibility of caring for her children, Donna went back to being the girl who came home from Virginia. Live fast and fly high. She could out-drink, out-smoke, and out-last any partier in the room, and more often than not that's what she did.

She never mentioned Charlie, but when the news came that he'd remarried she spent the next three days partying harder than ever.

"Do you want to talk about it?" I asked.

Donna shook her head. "Nope. What's done is done."

I wished she'd cry, not because I wanted to see her sad but because I hoped she'd unlock that dam of misery and let it wash away.

"You might feel better if you get this off your chest," I said.

"I feel fine," Donna replied. Then she pulled on a pair of skintight jeans and headed to the Crab House where they were supposedly having a disco dance contest. I tagged along.

We weren't there five minutes when Donna grabbed a guy standing at the bar and said, "Come on, let's dance."

They won the contest, and she came home with a bottle of champagne and a six-inch tall trophy.

"Man, that was fun," she said, then stretched out on the sofa.

We stayed at Mama's that night, and when I came downstairs in the morning Donna was having a glass of champagne and a cigarette for breakfast.

"What's this?" I asked.

Donna didn't answer, and Mama, standing behind her, just rolled her eyes.

The Call

The call comes four years after Donna moved to Baltimore.

When I answer Mama says, "Donna's got to go to the hospital for a procedure, and I'm too nervous to take her by myself. You've got to come down."

"What kind of procedure?" I ask.

"She's having trouble breathing," Mama answers. Her voice has that nervous high-pitched sound.

"Trouble breathing?" I repeat. This is news to me. I talk to Donna every week or two, and she hasn't mentioned anything about this. "Are you sure?"

"Dammit, Bette, I know what I'm talking about!"

"But I talked to her last week, and she didn't say anything about—"

"'Cause she doesn't want you to know," Mama argues. "She doesn't want anybody to know. Just me.

She wants to keep smoking those damn cigarettes and worry me into my grave, that's what she wants!"

"Oh, I don't think—"

"Well, you're not here!" Mama snaps.

I have no answer for that because it's true; I'm not there.

"I'll drive down this afternoon," I say.

"Well, hurry up and get started," Mama says.

I can almost feel the fear in her voice.

MAMA WAS NEVER THE same after she spent six months thinking Donna might be dead. All that worry caused her to shatter like a plate dropped on a tile floor. Even after Donna came home safe and sound, Mama stayed broken.

For months on end she tried to glue herself back together, but it never quite happened. There were slivers of heart and chucks of determination that were gone forever. You hear that time heals all wounds, but it didn't heal Mama's.

She still needs someone to lean on. Needing someone alongside of her is a lot like that plastic bottle of rye whiskey; she doesn't like it but it's something she has to have.

I DRIVE TO MARYLAND alone, all the while thinking, *She's my sister, so why wouldn't she tell me if something was wrong?* It starts to rain before I hit the turnpike and continues all the way to Baltimore.

IT'S STILL RAINING THE next morning when Mama and I take Donna to the hospital. As we drive crosstown I ask Donna why she hasn't told me about this.

"It's nothing to worry about," she says, but I can hear the thick rasp in her voice. How long has it been this way, I wonder. And why hadn't I heard it before? Even as I listen to her say it's nothing, I know better and I hate myself for not noticing sooner.

Once Donna is admitted, we settle into the waiting room. It's a dreary place with outdated magazines and a television no one watches. Only one other person is in the room. He is an old man with a thin top of white hair. The fingers of his hands drum against each other as he leans forward, his elbows resting on his knees. I can't help but wonder who he is waiting for. A wife perhaps. Although this is none of my business I find that thinking of this stranger and his troubles, helps me to move away from ours. For a brief moment I stop asking myself why I never noticed the sandpapered sound of my sister's voice.

I turn to my mother. "Can I get you anything?"

"No, thanks," she says, trying not to appear nervous; but I know better. We have been there a little more than two hours and she has rearranged the contents of her purse three times, folding and refolding her lace-trimmed handkerchief.

I thumb through the pile of magazines, pick up a dog-eared issue of *Woman's Day*, and hand it to Mama. "Would you like to look at this?"

"No, thanks," she says again. "I've got to clean out this purse, it's a mess."

"Okay." I replace the magazine, get up, and walk to the window. It's still raining. The flat cold gray of the sky fades into a darker gray horizon, and I try to push back the thought that it is the type of day to promise tragedy.

"Please, God," I pray, "don't let it be Donna." Before I return to my seat, I say another prayer asking God to spare the old man's wife also.

As soon as I sit down Mama says, "We've been waiting for over two hours, seems like we should've heard something by now." She pulls a bunch of credit cards from her wallet and starts rearranging them. When the Sears card falls to the floor, she turns to me. "Get that, will you? Then go ask if there's any news."

"I just did," I answer.

"That was twenty minutes ago!"

I can see how nervous Mama is, so I do as she asks. The receptionist says the same thing she said last time. "Doctor Craig will be down to see you as soon as he is out of surgery."

I tell Mama what the nurse said and again ask if she'd like something to read.

"No," she answers, then flips open her rearranged wallet. "But I could use a new picture of you three girls." She shows me an empty glassine pocket. "I took out that old photograph of Cousin Bessie. She hasn't called me in two years, so why should I bother carrying around her picture?"

Before Donna ran away, Mama would look a problem in the eye and go at it. Now she does as she's done with Bessie's photograph. She sets it aside, removes it from sight, and tells herself it's not something worth worrying about. Knowing this, I nod my acceptance. "When I get home, I'll look through my album and find a picture for you."

"Just don't forget."

"I won't."

"Okay."

Mama puts the wallet back in her purse and says, "I need to stretch my legs."

We get up and walk outside where we can stand under an awning. Searching for words to fill the emptiness, I say, "This weather is miserable." I pull a pack of cigarettes from my pocketbook and light one.

Mama says, "I'll have one too."

This astounds me. I have never seen her smoke. Never. I pull the pack out and give her one. She puts the cigarette between her lips, and I touch the flame of my lighter to it.

"I've never seen you smoke."

"I haven't for years," she answers, "but I'm real nervous today."

As I draw a second and third puff of nicotine into my lungs, thoughts of Donna's labored breathing and raspy voice come to mind. When I can't rid myself of the image, I snuff out the cigarette. Mama slowly finishes hers. The cigarette is like her rye whiskey; it fills the empty spots of who she used to be.

Another two hours pass before the short, dark-haired doctor comes into the waiting room. He is no longer wearing his operating room scrubs; he has changed into a navy blue business suit. He sits in the chair beside us and speaks in a soft, almost apologetic tone of voice.

"Unfortunately, Donna had a lot more problems than we anticipated," he says. "We had to do a tracheostomy."

Mama gasps.

"Do you know what that is?" the doctor asks.

I say, "Yes."

Mama answers, "No."

He removes his glasses and looks to Mama's face. "Donna has quite a bit of scar tissue on her bronchial cords, and it's restricting her ability to breathe. That, combined with the emphysema, prevents her from getting enough oxygen into her lungs."

"Donna has emphysema?" I repeat. This is the first I've heard of it.

"Severe emphysema," Doctor Craig replies. "To enable her to breathe we had to bypass that scar tissue, so we made an opening in the front of her throat and inserted a device to keep her airway open."

"Will she be all right now?" Mama asks.

"She'll be able to breathe, but not speak."

I listen and wait. I know what a tracheostomy is, and it seems somehow impossible he can be speaking of my devil-may-care sister. I want to call him a liar, but I only ask, "Is this permanent?"

"It's difficult to say." Doctor Craig pauses a moment. "With the tracheostomy she won't be able to smoke anymore, which will help with the emphysema, and she'll be able to suction out the congestion in her throat. If the fluid in her lungs clears, there's a possibility she can eventually have the scar tissue removed and the tracheostomy reversed."

"If that happens, will she be able to talk again?" I realize this is a dumb question, but it is all I have. I am searching for hope.

To avoid seeing our desperation, Doctor Craig looks down at the glasses in his hand as he speaks. "If we reverse the tracheostomy, Donna will be able to talk in a somewhat normal voice. But," he says with considerable emphasis on the word, "she's done a lot of damage to her throat and lungs. At this point I don't know whether it's reparable."

"What's the long-term prognosis?" I ask.

The truth is I don't want to hear what I am afraid is coming. For a moment I want to be like Mama. I want to close my eyes to this tragedy and swallow gulps of rye whiskey to dull the sorrow of reality.

Doctor Craig rubs the bridge of his nose then replaces his glasses. "The likelihood is that Donna will never live to be an old woman." He avoids looking at either of us when he says this, and then with the worst of the ugliness out of the way he lifts his eyes to Mama and says, "But rest assured, we will make certain Donna is kept comfortable for however long she has."

"However long she has?" Mama gasps. She starts to cry. Soft sobs bring forth a flow of tears that forces her to use her lace hankie.

I wrap my arm around Mama's shoulders. "Don't worry," I say, knowing such a thing is not possible. "Donna's strong, she can beat this."

Mama takes my hand in hers and says nothing. She is simply holding on to whatever she can, and right now I am it.

"When can we see her?" Mama asks.

"Donna is still in recovery." Doctor Craig suggests we go have lunch. "By then she should be back in her room."

I take Mama by the arm and lead her away. Neither of us speaks. It is as if we are walking through a bad dream, one from which we will wake and find it to be nothing more than the aftermath of a late-night pizza. In the span of a few hours it seems as if the world has changed. Everything looks unfamiliar. Even the green hallways appear narrower and headed in different directions. Clinging to one another, we walk to the end of the hallway and step into the elevator. On the ground floor there is a small coffee shop and we go in.

I cannot remember what we ordered; I remember only that we did not eat whatever it was. And I also remember Mama tearing her napkin into tiny shreds, nervously picking it apart piece by piece until there was nothing left but a scattering of scraps.

When we finally get to see Donna, she is pale and confused. Several times she tries to speak, but the words are no longer there. They have been replaced by a gurgle that starts in her chest and is then held prisoner by the steel fixture tied to her throat. I make a feeble effort to cheer her by saying it might only be temporary. She in turn pretends to believe me.

Donna doesn't cry. She never cries. Whatever sorrow Donna feels remains trapped inside of her. She mouths the words, "I guess this means I'm not going to be smoking for a while." She then gives a so-what shrug.

We stay beside her for another two hours, and as we turn to leave I hear the gurgling coming from her open airway. I can still remember the sound.

THE AFTERMATH

We have entered into a time of life when we are all liars. We lie to one another, and we pretend to believe the lies. Not only do we believe them, we pass them on as truths. I tell Mama that Donna will be okay. I say she just needs time to let her throat heal and then the tracheostomy will be reversed.

"You know Donna." I say, "She's tough. She can do it."

Mama pretends to believe me. She nods, but the fear never leaves her eyes.

When I ask Donna if she is uncomfortable or if there is something she needs, she shakes her head and grimaces. I know the look; it is her "Don't be such a sissy" expression. As I said, we are all liars.

Two days later Donna comes home from the hospital, and that afternoon medical supply trucks start arriving at her apartment. They come with a machine that growls and churns as it sucks loose the accumulation of mucus. They bring oxygen tanks that stand nearly as tall as me and cartons filled with gauze, tubing, and bottles of saline water. Donna sits in the recliner as Mama and I push chunks of furniture aside to make way for the barrage of medical supplies. In her bedroom the nightstand is turned sideways so we can squeeze in the chest that was moved to make way for boxes. The apartment was small to begin with and now it is overcrowded. It has the jumbled look of a storage bin.

"Maybe we should try to find you a bigger place," I suggest.

Again Donna shakes her head and gives me that same disdainful grimace. This time it is accompanied by a wave of her hand pushing the thought away.

I REMAIN IN BALTIMORE for another week, and during that week I learn what Donna's life will be like. She is a woman with a boyfriend and countless friends, yet she has told no one of this situation. The phone rings constantly, but Donna waves me off when I start to answer. Instead we wait until the caller leaves a message, and then we listen to it. Don, her boyfriend, has called twenty or more times. At first it is just a message for her to call him back. Then his messages become more desperate. "Dammit, Donna," he says.

"I'm worried about you! Call me back!"

Don doesn't even know Donna was in the hospital. She is a person who shares good times and fun. She is not a person who shares her fears and heartaches.

"Let me call him," I say. "He's really worried about you."

For the first several days, she simply gives a negative shake of her head then finally she writes a note and hands it to me. The note reads, *Call Don & tell him I don't want to see him anymore. Don't tell him about the tracheostomy.*

"I can't do that!" I say.

She points to the phone and nods.

"You've been dating him for over six months," I remind her. "He's not going to believe you just don't want to see him."

She takes the notepad and starts writing. The notepad is always with her; it is our way of communicating anything that can't be said with a nod, a shake of the head, or a wave of her hand. This time she writes *Tell him I'm involved with someone else, and it wouldn't be fair to keep seeing him. DO IT NOW!*

Not happy about doing this, I dial Don's number. Fortunately his answering machine picks up. I leave the message, but I am not a good liar and my words sound like a bad recording.

Afterward Donna settles into her recliner and watches television. There is little else to do. Although she has never been outside the United States, she watches travelogues of France, Italy, Greece, and faraway places I have never heard of.

At four-thirty I call and order a pizza for our dinner. She has no appetite and neither do I, so pizza sounds good. Fifteen minutes later the buzzer sounds, and I push the button to allow the deliveryman to enter the building. When I open the door it's not the pizza; it's Don. He angrily pushes past me and into the living room where Donna sits in the recliner.

"What the hell is –" He sees Donna and stops short.

She turns her head and waves him off. This is how Donna now dismisses anyone or anything she doesn't want to deal with.

Don turns to me. "What happened?"

I give him the whole story: the hospital, the surprise tracheostomy, and the fact that it has to stay in until her throat heals. Again I lie.

"Hopefully it won't be too long," I say.

Don walks across and kneels next to Donna's chair. "You're not getting rid of me so easily," he says. He takes her hand is his, but she is like a stick of wood. She allows him to take her hand, but she does not move into the embrace he offers. He tells her how she should trust that he would love her no matter what the circumstances.

"This is a temporary thing," he says. "We'll get through it together."

Donna looks at him, raises her eyebrows, and

crooks the right side of her mouth into an expression of doubt.

Don stays for nearly an hour, and we fill the time with small talk and watching bits of the detective show Donna has on television. When the pizza arrives Don doesn't eat but says he'll have a drink if there is any scotch in the house.

"No scotch," I say. "But we've got rye." It is the bottle Mama keeps on hand. Mama and Donna both drink rye whiskey now. Rye mixed with Coca Cola.

Don says yes to the rye, then drinks it quickly and leaves.

THE NEXT DAY DON sends flowers. He calls every day but doesn't come back during the week I am there. I mention this to Donna, and she gives me a thumbs up. It is a hand signal that requires no writing. Although Donna claims she is tired of him anyway, I know that is not the truth. The truth is that she is unwilling to make her misfortune someone else's problem.

I say, "Give the guy a chance. He's trying to do the right thing."

Donna gives me a scrunched up look of doubt and shakes her head. A few seconds later she takes the notepad and writes, *Not love. More like drinking buddies.*

In an odd way I realize that is probably true. Everybody loves Donna, but few people ever know the whole person. I do and her daughter Debi does. Mama is only a maybe, and although Geri is our sister she was always the baby so she never really had the chance to know Donna as I have.

Don't misunderstand me; they both love Donna and would do most anything for her, but with Mama it's a love-hate relationship. It's been that way ever since Donna ran off. As much as she loves Donna, there's a grain of unforgiving stuck in Mama's heart.

DON SOON TELLS THEIR friends at the Crab House about Donna's situation, and the get-well cards start pouring in. Many of them call even though they know she cannot speak. They leave warmhearted messages and say they will stop by. A few do, but when Donna peers from the side window and sees who is standing at the building entrance she shakes her head and I know not to answer.

She allows one friend to come in. It's Henrietta, a black woman who works with her at the bank. I wonder why Henrietta is the exception, but as I watch them sit there and carry on a one-sided conversation I understand.

Henrietta is a woman who knows heartache. She is the mother of two children, both born with birth defects. As she talks I learn her older boy has Down's syndrome, and the younger one who is seven years old has yet to speak. It is easy to see why she and my sister are such close friends; their lives run in parallel lines.

They both carry a burden heavier than many can even imagine. I look at Henrietta and see parts of her that indicate she is a young woman, but the slump of her body and the weariness in her eyes tell another story.

BEFORE I GET READY to leave on Friday, Debi arrives and a new brightness lights Donna's face. Her daughter is the one person who can bring about such a change. I know Donna loves her children equally, but Debi is the one she prefers to be with. Young Charlie has a male crustiness about him. He promises to visit, then doesn't show. If he does come, he flicks the television on and gives that his attention. Charlie is too much like his father. I doubt he knows how to reach inside his mother and pluck loose the things in her heart. Debi knows how. She and Donna are not simply mother and daughter; they're best friends.

Even though Debi has a job, she drops everything and comes when I tell her what has happened. When she arrives, I climb back into my car and start home to New Jersey. It is a long and tearful trip.

Coming Home

It is after nine o'clock when I pull into the garage, and I am weary to the bone. It is not the weariness of work but the weight of worry pressing down on me. As I turn into the drive I see the lights of our house aglow, and it warms my heart. The sight of it welcomes me home.

When Dick hears the garage door rumble up, he comes down the kitchen stairs to meet me. I have been gone nine days and he has had to shoulder the workload of running our ad agency alone, but he hasn't complained. He knows how painful this trip was and asks nothing of me. He steps aside and makes room for my sorrow. When I am ready to cry, his will be the shoulder I lean on. He is not only my husband, he is my greatest confidante.

"Hi, sweetheart," he says. "How was the trip?" He wraps his arms around me and squeezes me close.

"It was long," I say with a sigh. "I'm so tired."

This is painfully true. With Donna unable to speak, I forced myself to fill the voids with conversation. My mind never stopped. I reached out and grabbed bits of news, recalled memories of yesterdays, and laughed about long-forgotten friendships. The only thing I didn't speak of was her silence.

"Have you eaten dinner?" he asks.

"No, but I'm not hungry," I answer. The words are no sooner out of my mouth when I see the smile fade from his face. There is a foil-covered plate sitting on the back of the stove. He has dinner waiting for me.

Although I've given no thought to food, I feel warmed by his thoughtfulness.

"First I need a hot bath," I say. "After that I'll grab something to eat." I pretend not to notice the plate.

Dick's smile brightens again. "After that long drive, I thought you might be hungry. I baked a chicken breast and sweet potato. When you're out of the tub I'll heat it up."

"Oh, honey, how sweet." I kiss his cheek and head for the bathroom.

When the tub is filled with steaming water, I add two handfuls of jasmine bath crystals and pull my hair up in a rubber band twist. It looks more like a Brillo pad than a ponytail.

A bath is therapeutic. I take a shower to get clean; I take a bath to be rejuvenated. When the tub is full I step into it. The water is so hot it takes several minutes to ease myself into the froth of bubbles, and as I do my skin turns a rosy pink. For the first time in nine days I feel the muscles in my shoulders relax, so I lean back and let my head rest against the plastic pillow. Already I feel better on the outside, but the thoughts inside my head are still with me.

Worry makes my brain work overtime. When I'm at peace, thoughts fly in and out of my head like dandelion puffs carried off on a breeze. But troublesome thoughts take root and refuse to move on. They stay and pick at me with constant reminders of what I'm trying to forget.

I try to clear my mind by recalling the warmth of a summer day. I think of the lilac trees in the side yard and remember how fragrantly they will blossom in a few short months. For some odd reason the song "Blueberry Hill" comes to mind, and I hum a few bars of it. I haven't heard the song for ages, so why now? My thoughts slowly drift back to long-ago days. Days when Donna and I were both so young, still in school and still unsuspecting of the life ahead of us.

"Blueberry Hill" was her favorite song, and she could dance to it like no one else could. I picture her tight jeans wriggling across the gym dance floor to the bump-and-grind sound of Fats Domino and start to relive a night that is now a lifetime ago.

"**WOULDN'T YOU LOVE TO** go there?" Donna says.

"Go where?" I answer.

"Blueberry Hill."

Realist that I am, I chuckle. "Blueberry Hill isn't a real place. It's just a title somebody made up for this song."

Donna shrugs. "Believe what you want, but I know it's real."

THESE ARE GOOD MEMORIES. I try to hang on to them, wriggling my toes beneath the mound of bubbles and stretching my mind to recall what my favorite song had been. There is nothing. That memory is gone, and now I can recall only the chugging sound of her suctioning machine.

A GENTLE RAP ON the door shakes me from my reverie.

Dick calls out, "Honey, are you all right?"

"I'm fine," I answer, even though I am far from fine. I'm here and I want to be here, I need to be here. But I'm angry with myself, because I can't be in two places at once. I vacillate between great sympathy for what Donna is going through and a swell of anger that reminds me of how she ignored all the warning signs and allowed this to happen. Still, I say "I'm fine," because that's what you do. When someone asks how you are, you say *fine*, regardless of whether it's true.

Dick says, "You've been in there an hour."

"I'm unwinding," I answer. "I'll be out soon."

"Okay," he says. "As long as you're all right."

The sound of his footsteps tells me he is returning to the basketball game, and in a strange way I am glad to be left alone with my misery. Misery is not something to be shared. Just as Donna refused to share it with Don, I withhold it from Dick. Perhaps I do this because I know the sad truth is no matter how much I am loved, my husband can do nothing about the horror of this situation.

I HAVE BEEN IN THE tub so long the water has grown cold. It is no longer a comfort, so I pull the plug and step onto the bathmat. A soft flow of air from the heater warms the room. It is a sharp contrast to the frigid air in Donna's apartment. Although she lives south of here her building is poorly insulated, and the iciness of winter slides across the floor and settles in the air. The apartment is always cold. It's the kind of cold that goes through your skin and burrows into your bones.

Even so, Donna doesn't complain about her circumstances. Debi and I both asked her to come and live with us, but she refused.

I like my independence is what she wrote on her notepad.

If an intruder broke through the thin glass of Donna's apartment window she couldn't cry out for help. Without a voice, she can't even do something as small as ordering a pizza, so how can it be considered independence? I think the truth is my sister lives alone because she doesn't want to be a burden.

Perhaps if I were more insistent she'd change her mind.

I wonder if I accept her answer too readily because deep inside I am fearful of living with oxygen tanks and suctioning machines? They carry the sound and smell of sickness, and once experienced it is something that can never be forgotten.

Yes, they give life, but it comes packaged in heartache.

THE ONSET OF WINTER

It is an ugly day. Dark clouds push up against each other and hover low in the sky; not even a pinpoint of brightness shows through. Another storm is on the way. Yesterday's snow is already a hard crust of ice on the trees, and the street is a slippery mixture of mud and slush. Although the furnace here is chugging out a steady stream of hot air I shiver, thinking about Donna huddled beneath an afghan as she sits alone in her apartment.

The building she lives in is old. Old and drafty. The wind pushes against the window and passes through the towels tucked around the sill. For the millionth time I wish Donna was closer, close enough that I could drive over every afternoon and bring hot soup or a few minutes of friendship. Baltimore is less than two hundred miles away, but right now it feels as if it's on the other side of the earth.

I move aside a pile of papers, reach for the telephone, and punch in a sequence of numbers. My finger has barely left the last digit when the ring bounces back and closes the stretch of miles between us.

I listen and count, certain there will be no response until after the fourth ring. Finally the click comes, but the recorded voice is not Donna's. It belongs to her daughter. Debi sounds like her mother did a short time ago. Most callers don't realize it's the daughter speaking, not the mother. I do, but then I know the story.

Debi says no one is available to answer the call, then tells me to leave a message after the tone. As a long beep sounds in my ear I say, "Donna, it's me, Bette. Pick up if you're there."

Moments later I hear the second click and know my sister is on the line. For want of anything better to say, I ask, "Are you there?"

Tap.

"Is everything okay?"

Tap.

"Is anyone else there?"

Tap, tap.

I ask questions that can be answered with a yes or no, because those are the only answers she can give. A metal pen sits beside the telephone for use when I call. A single tap means yes, a double tap is no.

I continue with a steady stream of conversation about inconsequential things: a newspaper article I've read, a television show I've watched, and so on. I don't talk about books because Donna doesn't read. She loses herself in a television show the way I lose myself in a book.

It has been just two days since my last call and I have nothing new to say, but I talk anyway. I force myself to sound cheerful. This may be the only outside communication Donna has today, so I try to make it as pleasant as possible. I tell jokes that are older than Mama, poke fun at the day's headlines, and laughingly complain about the price of tomatoes. Occasionally my sister taps an affirmative agreement, but there is nothing else. The sound of her silence is painful beyond belief. When I say goodbye, I promise to come for a visit next week. As I am about to hang up I hear the smack of Donna's lips kissing the telephone receiver and understand it is her way of saying she loves me.

TWO DAYS LATER I receive a letter from Donna. Her letters are short and to the point. She is no fonder of writing than she is of reading.

Dear Bette, she writes. *When you come down please bring a bag of peanuts in the shell. I need them for the squirrels. Still no sign of Lucifer. I miss that damn cat and wish he'd come back. Tuesday the county nurse is taking me to Doctor Craig for my monthly checkup. Last time he said there was a possibility he might be able to reverse the tracheostomy if the scar tissue in my throat heals. Geri's birthday is coming up and I've not been able to get out to buy a present. Would you pick one up for me? Well, I'd better close for now, my hand is tired and I think this pen is running out of ink. Love you, Donna*

THE LETTER REMINDS ME of Donna's two squirrels. Every afternoon they come and wait alongside the rusted grill standing outside her patio door. They stay there until she slides the door open and places four peanuts atop the grill. They seem to understand the way this bounty is to be divided, and neither of the squirrels ever takes three. Donna has named them Sam and Susie, but their names remain unspoken.

Now that Lucifer, the cat, has run off, there are days when these two squirrels are Donna's only company. Mama comes over several times a week but not every day.

"I'm getting older," she says. "You can't expect me to be running over there every day."

No one argues with Mama anymore, because it is useless to do so. Arguing with her means one of two things will happen. Either she'll get mad and stop speaking to you for a good long while, or she'll get her feelings hurt and cry and when that happens you end up apologizing all over the place.

THINKING ABOUT LUCIFER GIVES me an idea, an idea that warms my heart as much as Brandi herself does. Brandi is the Bichon Frise sitting in my lap. She is my constant companion. She loves me when I am loveable and loves me just as much when I am impossible. This is a secret only dog lovers know: rubbing a dog's tummy brings peace of mind. I tell myself it is almost impossible to be sad, lonely, or depressed when you're petting the dog in your lap. Then I congratulate myself on having such wisdom and start calling the pet shops.

Eight numbers later, I am still asking the same question. When the woman at Framer's Pet Shop answers the telephone, I ask, "Do you have any Bichon puppies?"

"Not on hand," she says, "but if you want to place an order, I'm expecting two in about a month."

"Bichons are on back order?" I ask incredulously.

"Yes." She takes on a tone that infers this is the norm. "The litter is still too young to be sold. But if you want to leave a credit card deposit, I can reserve one for you."

I glance at the yellow pages where there are listings for another twenty or thirty pet shops. Reasonably sure I'll find one today, I say, "I'll think about it and let you know."

"Don't wait too long," she says. "They may be gone."

I hang up and dial the next pet shop, then the next,

and the next. This continues all morning until I get to Zelda's Pets. Like the first twenty-seven pet shops, she does not have a Bichon but sympathizes with my plight and gives me the telephone number of a friend who breeds Dalmatians.

"Maybe Klaus can suggest something," she tells me.

Since Zelda's is the final listing for pet shops, I have no choice but to call Klaus.

"Zelda thought maybe you can help me," I say, and I tell him what I am looking for.

He speaks with a heavy accent and acknowledges my words with "Ya, ya." Afterward I hear some indistinct mumbling and assume he is consulting with someone else. Apparently this is not the case, because he ultimately suggests, "Dalmatian make nice pet. For friend of Zelda I do small price. Is good, yes?"

"No, not good. I'm looking to get a dog for my sister, but her apartment is really, really small. She's sick and all alone," I say. I give him the entire story, most of which I am certain he neither understands nor cares about. Still, I feel if someone realizes how important this is, they'll help me find a dog. Klaus comes through and gives me the names of three places to call. One of these is the North Jersey Kennel.

The phone rings nine times before a man picks up and says, "This is Pete."

I cut to the chase and ask, "Do you have any Bichon puppies?"

"Yeah. Two."

"For sale right now?" My surprise is obvious.

"Yeah. Two Bichons and a Maltese."

This place is in Paterson, which is a good hour from our house, but now I'm like a hound in the hunt so I ask, "How late are you open?"

"Five-thirty."

I look at the clock: five-ten. As I fish under the desk for my shoes, I tell the guy Donna's story and plead with him to wait for me.

"I'm on my way right now," I say.

It's obvious this guy doesn't want to wait. "What's the rush? The same dogs will be here tomorrow."

"I've got to have this dog tonight," I exclaim. This makes no sense, even to me. Of course, I could go tomorrow. Except by now I am convinced these are the only two Bichons in the state of New Jersey. What if somebody breaks in during the night and steals them? Too risky! I whine and beg.

"Okay, okay." Pete finally agrees to wait for me, but adds, "Be careful driving, I don't want you killed on the way here." He laughs and hangs up.

As I grab my coat I hear the garage door rumble up and realize Dick is home from work. Chances are he's thinking, "What's for supper?" But I'm thinking, "He can drive." That way I can hold the dog on the way home.

With checkbook in hand, I'm down the stairs and sliding into the passenger seat before Dick has his key out of the ignition. "We've got to go to Paterson," I say with a sense of urgency.

"Why?"

"Hurry," I say, fastening my seat belt. "I'll explain on the way."

Without much of an argument, he puts the car in reverse, backs out of the garage, and heads for Route 287. I give the address of the kennel and explain the situation.

"I'm with Pete," Dick says. "Why can't you just get the dog tomorrow?"

It a rational question that requires a fairly rational answer, but I wave it off and repeat, "These are the last two Bichons in New Jersey!"

When we get to the kennel, everything is dark and the parking lot empty. I jump out of the car and run to the building. The door is locked. I panic and pound my fist against it shouting, "You said you'd wait!"

The light goes on and Pete bellows, "Okay, okay, I'm coming."

A round little man with mustard on his mustache opens the door and smiles at me. "You gotta be the lady that called. I'm Pete."

"Hi," I say sheepishly, now embarrassed by my behavior. "Thanks for waiting." I introduce Dick and myself, then the three of us start toward the back room. As we pass the office I see a half-eaten sandwich on what appears to be Pete's desk.

"Did we interrupt your dinner?"

"Nah. It's bowling night, but the guys are going to the Fish House. I'm not big on fish, especially clams. Oysters neither."

Pete opens a second door, and when he snaps on the light any number of yapping dogs spring to life. The room is wall-to-wall wire cages.

"Afraid I got some bad news," he says. "I thought I had two Bichons, but I got two Maltese."

The disappointment washes over me like sludge from a sewer. The heartache I feel for my sister and the frustration of this search rises like a lump in my throat.

"You don't have any Bichons?" I ask.

Apologetically he answers, "Just one. A male."

I let out a whoosh of disappointment. I have my heart set on a female Bichon. I came here hoping to find a dog exactly the same as the one I have. Brandi is a lap-sitting, kiss-giving, cuddle bug, and she brings me more joy than I ever thought possible. My goal is to find a dog that will bring the same joy to my speechless sister. Although I've been told there is just the one male, I say with a moan, "No females?"

Pete shakes his head. "I've got a female terrier."

"The male Bichon," I say, "is he old enough to sell right now?"

Pete nods. "That's him. Nine weeks today." He points to a cage in the third tier. Inside is a white ball of fluff sleepily curled around a rag toy.

This dog is not yapping like the others, so I think maybe a male dog will work after all.

I poke my finger through the wire mesh and talk to him as I stroke his paw. A little black eye pops open, and he begins wagging his tail. "Awww," I gush. It seems this one and only Bichon likes me, and if he likes me he's going to love Donna.

"Can we take him out of the cage?"

Pete puts the dog on the floor, and I sit down beside him. He starts climbing on my lap and licking my face.

"Adorable, isn't he?" I turn to Dick, but he's looking at a German shepherd puppy on the bottom row. I repeat, "This Bichon's adorable, isn't he?"

Still with the shepherd, Dick says, "Look at the paws on this guy. He's gonna be a big one."

Pete motions to the large black pup a few cages down. "That's nothing. Check this one out. Newfoundland; he'll be the size of a bear when he's full grown."

I interrupt them and ask, "How much?"

Pete eyes the ticket on the Newfoundland's cage and says, "Six hundred."

"Not him. This Bichon. How much is this Bichon?"

"Six fifty."

"Six hundred and fifty dollars?" Dick repeats. He hasn't said "overpriced" but it's there, hanging onto the tail of the question mark.

When people have been married a long time they start to know each other's thoughts, and I am pretty certain Dick is comparing the pound-for-pound cost of this dog and the Newfoundland.

I know this dog is way out of my budget. I know I'm going to have to cut back on any number of things to make up for such an expenditure. But by now the image of this Bichon sitting alongside my silent sister has settled into my mind.

"We'll take him," I say.

Pete warns, "He's not show quality."

This fact doesn't faze me. I'm not looking for a show dog. All I want is a companion for my sister. I want a living, breathing, loving thing that will save her from being lonely. But my pound-for-pound husband asks, "Why is he not show quality?"

Pete picks up the dog and turns its face to us. "Look at the eyes. Bichons are supposed to have a black rim around the eyes. This dog only has the black rim on one eye."

I look and, sure enough, the poor little thing has one perfect eye and one with an albino rim around it, giving him the appearance of pink eye. The dog wriggles loose from Pete and buries its head in my lap as if it's embarrassed by this abnormality. Now, more than ever, I am convinced this is the right dog. He and Donna will be two slightly impaired beings helping each other.

"We'll take him," I repeat.

Twenty minutes later all three of us are in the car and on our way home, Dick, the dog, and me. Only now do I realize that in the frenzy of this day I have forgotten to defrost something for dinner. Uh oh.

I suggest, "It's late; maybe we should pick up a pizza for supper."

"You forget to defrost something again?"

"Sort of." I start to defend my mistake. "Even if I had defrosted something, by the time I cook it would be midnight. How about Chinese?"

"Let's just go out for dinner."

"We can't."

"Why?"

"The dog." I hope this will be enough of an explanation, but it's obvious Dick wants more. "He's just a baby. We can't dump him in the house and leave. He and Brandi may not get along."

"They're the same kind of dog."

As I said, a wife usually knows her husband's mind. Right now I can almost guarantee Dick is thinking, *These are dogs we're talking about.* But without grumbling he agrees to Chinese, and I am relieved. When we arrive at Joy Chow he goes in for the food, and I stay in the car with the dog. Through the front window I can see Dick waiting patiently at the counter as the cook throws a handful of something in the wok.

I thank God for this man of infinite understanding. Sometimes in this life we get lucky. I did. Donna didn't. Once again I start to grow angry at the monster she married.

My thoughts fade when I see Dick returning to the car with two brown bags. I reach across and open the driver's side door. The dog wakes up and starts licking my face again. Dick reaches across and hands me the bags, and I set them on the floor. Little Mister Pink-eye goes crazy, sniffing, wagging, sniffing, moaning. Finally he lets out a desperate woof.

"He wants this food." I laugh and think about Brandi who gets a piece of everything I eat.

"Don't give him any," Dick warns. "He's a puppy. He'll get sick."

"I wasn't going to," I reply.

"Make sure. Otherwise he'll throw up all over the house."

Dick knows me as well as I know him. He knows that given the chance, I will spoil this dog with hand-fed snacks just as I've spoiled Brandi.

"Don't worry," I say, but even as the words come from my mouth, I am thinking I will dip my finger in the sauce and give him a taste. Brandi will get several chunks of General Tso's chicken, but the pup will have only a tiny taste.

After dinner and several finger licks of spare rib sauce, we settle in the family room. The puppy tries to climb into my lap, and Brandi swats him away. This is her territory, and she is not ready to give it up.

"He's just a baby," I say and move Brandi aside to make room for the pup. Eventually they settle down, Brandi next to me, Pink-eye in my lap.

When the basketball game ends, Dick clicks off the television and we start to bed.

"What are you going to do with the dog?" he asks.

"He can sleep in Brandi's bed." This seems like a good idea since Brandi doesn't use the bed; she sleeps with us.

Dick shakes his head. "Unh-unh. He's not trained. I don't want him running around the house."

Remembering the challenge of training Brandi, I don't argue.

Dick brings a laundry basket from the basement, and I line it with a thick terry towel. Then we head for the bedroom.

I set the laundry basket close to my side of the bed and lower him into it. For a while he's content, but the minute he sees Brandi jump on the bed he gets restless. He starts pawing the sides of the basket. He wants out. He wants me to pick him up again. He wants to be where Brandi is, and she wants nothing to do with him.

I feel sorry for the dog; he is small and alone. Like my sister he is flawed and in need of company. I sit on the floor beside the basket and pet him until he finally falls asleep.

At last I am in bed. I close my eyes, listen to the soft sound of puppy snores, and imagine Donna clapping her hands in a wordless call for Pink-eye to come. I can see him winking his albino eye as he leaps into her arms.

THE GIFT

Saturday morning I start to think about the ramifications of owning a dog. Feeding will be easy enough, but there's also the training and walking. Neither of which Donna can handle.

It took me almost a year to get Brandi completely housebroken. Now I've got only a few days to train this pup. I convince myself it can be done. I plan to take the dogs out together figuring once Pink-eye sees Brandi get a reward for piddling, he'll catch on quickly. There's just one problem: the pup wants to be with Brandi and Brandi keeps pushing her off. I take them out together anyway.

Brandi circles the yard with Pink-eye right behind nosing her butt. Nothing happens. Neither dog does anything, so I bring them inside. I put the pup back in the laundry basket and take Brandi out alone. She immediately does what she came to do. I mark the spot, switch Brandi for the pup, and head back out. I sit Pink-eye on the marked spot, and he starts to sniff. When he decides to wander away, I herd him back to the spot and wait.

Again today the sky is gray and the wind cold. "Hurry up," I say, but the pup ignores me. Eventually it starts to drizzle, and when I am just about ready to give up on teaching this dog anything he squats and pees. I "good boy" him all over the place and give him two cookies.

The next day I take the two dogs out together again. This time it's a bit better. The pup follows Brandi's lead, only he squats like she does instead of lifting his leg. Nothing's perfect.

By Saturday morning Pink-eye is partly trained. I've got a length of chain that clicks onto his collar and a stake Dick will pound into the ground. All Donna has to do is slide the patio door open and hook him up. Problem solved.

As we roll down Route 95, I tell Dick, "Donna knows we're coming."

"Good," he answers.

"But she doesn't know about the dog."

He turns and looks at me. "You spent six hundred-and-fifty dollars, and you don't even know if she wants a dog?"

"Why would she not want it?"

"It's a lot of responsibility."

"It's also a lot of company," I rationalize. "She loves Brandi, so why would she not love this dog?"

"Six hundred-and-fifty dollars," Dick repeats and shakes his head.

"That's how much Bichons cost."

"If you're not sure she wants a dog, you should've gotten a rescue."

He may have a point here, but I simply say, "What's done is done."

Not ready to concede, Dick asks, "What if the cat comes back?"

"He won't. He's been gone too long." I don't bother to say the missing Lucifer was what prompted me to buy the dog. And the chain.

For the remainder of the trip it is mostly small talk. Dick listens to a basketball game on the radio until it turns to static and fades away. I wrestle with the dogs, trying to get Brandi and Pink-eye to settle down.

WHEN WE PULL INTO the parking space in front of her apartment, the living room blind is halfway up and I can see Donna sitting in the chair beside the window. She leans forward and rubs a patch of frost from the windowpane. I know she is watching for us, and as soon as I step to the entranceway the buzzer sounds. I open the door and the two dogs dash in. I have a leash for the pup but I don't use it, because Brandi follows me and the pup follows Brandi.

I see Donna standing in the open door as soon as we turn down her corridor. The dogs run ahead of us. Brandi knows where we are going because she's been here countless times before; the pup just goes wherever Brandi goes.

By the time we get to the door Donna is laughing at the dogs. In a sign language of our own making, she points to me then holds up two fingers and mouths the words, *You have two dogs now?*

"Not me," I say and shake my head.

She points to the dogs, spreads her hands, and shrugs.

I understand the question, and I'm trying to hold back a grin. "Brandi's my dog. The other one is yours."

Donna's eyes go wide. She points to her own chest and mouths a single word. *Mine?*

I nod.

In less than a heartbeat my sister, still hooked to her oxygen tank, is on the floor playing with the dog. He scrambles onto her lap and kisses her face. Donna laughs like I have not seen her laugh in many months. It's not the kind of laugh you can hear. It's a muted chuffing sound. But I see the motion of laughter in her bony shoulders. When she finally looks up and silently thanks me, there is a river of tears running down her face and I know it was the best six hundred-and-fifty dollars I will ever spend.

LATER THAT AFTERNOON I call Mama and ask her to come over.

"I'm doing the laundry," she says. "Floyd's out of underwear."

"So come when you finish. Donna's got something to show you."

"I don't know…"

"Come on, Mama, this is exciting."

She hesitates again.

"Bring Floyd," I say. "Dick can get take out from Nino's, and we'll have dinner together."

"Too much garlic in that stuff. It gives Floyd heartburn."

"Okay, we'll get Chinese."

"I don't think so," Mama says. "Floyd doesn't like being in a crowd. Everybody talking at one time throws his hearing aid off."

"There's no crowd," I say. "It's just Dick and me." Before she has time to come up with another excuse, I remember their weakness and suggest, "We could get black pepper crabs. How's that?"

She finally agrees but adds, "We can't stay all evening. Floyd likes to be home in time to see *Wheel of Fortune*."

Two hours later the doorbell rings, and Mama is standing there alone. "Floyd decided not to come. He asked me to bring him back a couple of crabs. The noise of everybody talking—"

"Bothers his hearing aid," I say. I don't argue

because there is nothing to be gained by it. Floyd is older than Mama, and living with him has caused her to be older than her years.

When Mama steps inside, Pink-eye comes running over and starts barking.

He has not only settled in but now this is his house, his property to safeguard. He is no longer just a dog, he is *the watchdog* and this is a stranger.

"What's wrong with Brandi?" Mama asks as I push the five-pound terror from her pathway.

"That's not Brandi." I smile. "It's Donna's new dog."

"Donna's dog?" Mama looks at the dog and frowns. "Good Lord."

"What's the problem?"

"Your sister can barely take care of herself. How in the name of God is she supposed to walk a dog?"

"She doesn't have to." I take Mama to the sliding glass door and show her the stake. "See? All Donna has to do is clip the chain to the dog's harness. Then he can be outside as much as he wants. She won't have to walk him or worry about him running away."

"We'll see," Mama replies skeptically and lowers herself onto the sofa. She looks at Donna sitting in the recliner, the dog curled in her lap. "Are you sure you want that? Taking care of a dog is a lot of work."

Donna furrows her eyebrows and nods an emphatic yes. She flutters her hand over her heart and motions to the dog, meaning she loves him.

Mama heaves a sigh that would have you believe

she's got the weight of the world on her shoulders. "Well, I'm too old to walk it for you, so I hope you know what you're doing."

WHEN DICK RETURNS WITH the crabs we put two aside for Floyd, then tear open the bag to divide up the remainder along with the coleslaw and piping hot French fries. I look at Donna's plate. It is painfully sparse. She has only a small handful of fries. And she's feeding some of those to the dog.

After dinner the three of us play rummy while Dick watches a basketball game on television. Donna holds the dog in her lap and shows him each card as it's dealt, but Pink-eye pays no attention. He licks his paw and cleans the French fry grease from his face. Three times in a row Donna slaps down a winning hand and goes out, racking up points while Mama and I get caught holding a slew of cards in our hand.

The minute Donna smacks down that third hand, Mama gets a pouty mouth and says, "I've got to go home. Floyd's waiting for his crabs."

The real reason she wants to leave is because she's losing. If Mama was up a couple hundred points, Floyd could starve to death before she'd go home.

As she's saying goodbye, I grab my jacket and tell her, "I'll walk you out."

Mama has parked at the far end of the lot where there are no other cars. As we start down the long walkway I sneak a glance at her face, yellowed by the glow of a dim streetlight. The laugh lines are gone, and crevices of worry have taken over. It seems as though the years have suddenly rushed in and settled upon her. Not slowly as you might expect to happen, but pow! Like a pie in the face. One day she was a dark-haired mother with kids squabbling over the roller skate key, and then suddenly she's an old woman stooped under the weight of sickness and survival.

"I don't know," she says, shaking her head sorrowfully. "I think getting this dog's a bad idea."

I wrap my arm around her shoulders. "Try to be patient. Having a dog is good for Donna. She's lonely, she needs something—"

"Don't you think I know she's lonely?" Mama flares up like a Fourth of July rocket. "I'm the one who comes over here three, maybe four times a week. I'm the one who checks she's got groceries. I'm the one..."

Mama's voice is thick with a mix of anger and guilt. Guilt because she urged Donna to move to a place where she is far from her sisters and children. Anger because now Mama feels it's her responsibility to care for Donna. The irony of this is that my sister isn't sorry she moved to Baltimore, and she doesn't want anyone taking care of her.

I've told Mama that a number of times, but it's not something she wants to hear. Once she gets in a feeling-sorry-for-herself mood, the only thing you can do is appease her.

"I know how much you do," I say. "And we all appreciate it."

"Just so long as you understand," Mama grumps, and we keep walking. When we reach her car, she struggles with the lock and I offer to help.

"I can do it myself!"

As the big Ford Fairlane pulls away, I watch how Mama cranes her neck to look over the steering wheel. She is once again getting smaller. At one time she was a formidable force; now she is a tiny woman with more responsibility than she can handle.

When I return to the apartment Donna is in the recliner, suctioning her throat. The dog is asleep in her lap. I ask if she's decided on a name for him.

She nods and hands me a scrap of paper where she has written a single word.

I read what she has handed me. "Jason?"

She nods, gives me a mischievous grin, and mouths the words, *I'll tell you about it sometime.*

I laugh. "Okay, Jason he is." I can't help but think how sad it is that the dog will never hear his mistress speak the name she has given him. He has learned to come when he hears the sound of the cricket clicker I have given her.

Winter's End

I wish I could tell you this is a short story, but it's not. Like many of life's miseries it stretches itself out, making hours into days and weeks into months. In the bitter cold we drive the icy roads back and forth to Baltimore, sometimes every third week, sometimes once a month. It is a four-hour drive, so we leave early Saturday morning and return home late Sunday evening. Often the laundry goes undone, and the dust on the dining room table is left to thicken until the grain of the wood is no longer visible.

These things no longer bother me. I have come to realize they are small. They are actually smaller than small: they are miniscule. Several times a week I call Donna; I talk and she taps. I tell myself it is not much but it's better than nothing.

When we visit I see the weariness in Mama's face. It is not the weariness of work; it's the weariness of worry. From time to time Mama and Donna will have a spat and go for days without seeing each other. I always know when this happens because Mama will call me and say I ought to check up on Donna. She doesn't mention them having an argument, but I know.

All winter we take turns visiting. Dick and I go some weekends, Geri and Ted go other weekends, and Debi goes more often than anyone. We schedule it on our calendar, the same as we'd schedule any other responsibility.

JUST WHEN I START to believe winter will never end, bits of yellow pop out on the wisteria bushes. The coming of spring seems to soften the harshness of winter. It is as if the weight of snow and ice has been lifted from my chest and I can breathe again. I wonder if my sister is experiencing this feeling.

That same week I receive her letter. This letter is just as short as her others, but this one has happiness woven through ever word. Debi is getting married.

Please come down, she writes. *We need to go shopping for a dress.*

For the first time in many months, I can feel the happiness in my sister's soul.

THAT WEEKEND WHEN WE arrive in Baltimore, I can almost swear Donna looks healthier. She has a blush in her cheeks and seems less dependent upon the oxygen. There are periods that stretch as long as forty minutes before she slides the tubing back under her nose and breathes.

The portable tank holds two hours of oxygen. It goes with us on our shopping expeditions. For these excursions Donna pulls on the skinny jeans that now hang loose like trousers and fluffs a sheer scarf around her neck to hide the chunk of metal in the front of her throat. Dressed as she is and with makeup on her face, she looks pretty. I smile and say, "You look great."

She shrugs and gives me the cynical look of doubt that is hers alone. She mouths the words, *I'm trying.*

When we arrive at the mall I get a wheelchair for Donna. Not because she can't walk, but because the mall stretches out for almost a mile and the oxygen tank is too heavy to carry. The first trip we are there for almost three hours, and only twice does she need to reach for the oxygen. On that first trip Mama finds a dress that falls in soft folds over the areas she wants to hide. When she steps out of the dressing room, Donna claps her hands and gives a thumbs up.

In the short span of less than a year, I have learned to read my sister's lips and her movements. So has Mama. We have come to understand these things almost as well as others understand the spoken word. Donna makes no effort to talk to the salespeople or the waiter at the restaurant. She has already indicated what she wants, and I order for her. Were you to pass by and see the three of us at the lunch table, you would believe we are as normal as everyone else. Our heartache doesn't show, and neither does my sister's tracheostomy. Even though Donna doesn't find a dress this day, it is a good one.

IT TAKES SEVERAL SUCH trips, but in time Donna finds a dress. The moment she puts it on I think how lovely she looks. She smiles and nods. If she had words we would have squealed with delight. She would have asked me time and time again if the back was too snug around her butt or if the color was wrong, but as it is we must settle for a single nod. "You look absolutely beautiful!" I say, and it is the truth.

Donna has chosen a cocktail length dress of silver blue lace. The body of the dress is lined, but the sleeves and mandarin collar that rises to hide her throat are lace. It is enough to cover the tracheostomy and yet allow for the passage of air to breathe. The dress is narrow through the waist and hips, but the below that there is a swirl of skirt to camouflage her thinness. She is ready to be the mother of the bride.

TWO DAYS BEFORE THE wedding Donna and Mama come to stay at our house. Donna drives. The back of her car is loaded with equipment: the big oxygen tank, the portable oxygen tank, boxes of saline solution, the suctioning machine, countless medications, boxes of supplies, and the dress.

On Saturday we arrive at the church. Donna walks with her back straight and her chin high. We are seated in the first pew and only then do I start to wonder if Charlie will come with Cyndi Lou, who is now his wife. I glance at my sister and pray he doesn't. I know it has been years but I also know in the secret part of her heart, the part where Donna hides the pain of life, she still loves him. Simply saying this prayer causes me to remember how much I detest the man. Remembering how he loves himself and with such vanity, I fear he will indeed come with Cyndi Lou hanging on his arm.

I sit at an angle where it appears I am facing forward, but I can in fact see the church entrance. I watch and wait. Only a few minutes pass before Charlie walks in. He comes alone. I breathe a sigh of relief.

With nothing more than a nod, Charlie slides into the pew behind us.

After the ceremony there is a reception. As is customary, the bride and groom have the first dance; then the bride dances with her father and the groom with his mother. Then they call for a dance by the bride's parents.

Charlie comes to our table and extends his hand to Donna. She smiles and accepts it as if it is perfectly normal for them to dance together. He leads her onto the dance floor, and they sway to the beat of a slow fox trot. As I watch Donna gracefully glide across the floor, a swell of admiration rises in my throat. I have never felt more proud of my sister than I do at that moment. No one in the room, save myself, knows the agony she feels.

When the dance ends, I make my way to her side and we go outside to her car where she can clear the phlegm that has collected in her airway. As we walk across the parking lot, I hear the gurgling in her throat and see a damp stain appear on the lace collar of her dress. I hand her a tissue, and she quickly blots the moist spot. She slides behind the wheel and turns on the ignition. It seems ironic that the converter enabling her to operate the suction machine works off the cigarette lighter.

Twenty minutes later we return to the reception, but for Donna the dancing is over. For the remainder of the evening she moves slowly, nodding graciously at the other guests, smiling but not speaking.

Before we leave I have a chance to talk with Debi, and I say it's good that her dad didn't bring his wife. Debi, who in many ways has grown to be like Donna, frowns.

"Are you kidding?" she says. "I told Daddy that if Cyndi Lou shows up anywhere near the wedding, I'd have him thrown out!"

I hug my niece to my chest and whisper, "Thank you." I want to say *Bless your heart, honey, you're just like Donna,* but I don't because it sounds too much like Mama.

When the Leaves Fall

All too soon the summer is gone and other than Debi getting married, little has changed. This life of hoping for change is painful in more ways than it is possible to count. I think it is because our expectations have risen. During the months prior to the wedding and even for a short while afterward, Donna seemed somehow better. More alive. Happier. But with the coming of winter, that happiness has waned.

A month or so after I have packed away my summer dresses and thoughts of warm sunny days, I get a telephone call from Debi.

"Hi, Aunt Bette," she says. Her voice is exceptionally cheerful.

"You sound happy," I say.

"I am," she answers. "You're going to be a great aunt."

Not immediately catching the inference of what she's said I laugh. "I thought I already was a great aunt."

"No." Debi stretches the word out, slowing the conversation. "I mean you are going to be a Great Aunt!"

When she puts emphasis on the word "great" I suddenly catch on. "Oh my goodness! You're having a baby?"

"Yes," she giggles.

The usual barrage of questions follows: When is the baby due? Do you know if it's a boy or girl? And most importantly, does your mom know? When Debi and I talk, my sister becomes her mom.

Debi laughs. "Of course Mom knows. Jim and I went down this weekend and told her."

"She must be so excited."

"Excited is hardly the word for it. We went shopping, and she bought a whole bunch of yarn so she could start crocheting a baby blanket."

We talk for a while, and before I hang up I realize this will not be a terrible winter.

DONNA ONLY KNOWS HOW to crochet one thing: granny squares. I imagine by this time she has ten, maybe twelve squares waiting to be hooked together. That same afternoon I call her, and I talk for almost twenty minutes with her tapping out answers. When I ask how many squares she has made she taps out the number, but there are so many taps I lose count.

"Eleven?" I guess.

Tap, tap.

"More?"

Tap.

"Fourteen?"

Tap, tap.

We continue through this game until I hit seventeen, and then I get a single tap. "You've got seventeen squares done?" I laugh. "You can slow down, the baby's not due until April."

I hear the chuff of her laughter.

When we finally hang up I feel the surge of expectation returning. Once again I believe something good will happen. I believe my sister will get well. Maybe not the dancing, drinking, partying woman she once was but well enough to have this chunk of metal removed from her throat. Donna can do it, I tell myself. She's strong, she's tough, and she's going to be a grandma.

THAT CHRISTMAS WE CELEBRATE like never before. The whole family comes to our house. They arrive on Christmas Eve and stay until the day after Christmas. Mama and Donna drive up from Maryland, and this time Floyd comes even though there will be a crowd.

"Don't expect he'll answer anything you ask,"

Mama says, "because he's not wearing his hearing aid."

When we sit down to dinner on Christmas Eve Donna sits next to Debi, who is now full and round. Dick says grace, and we thank the Lord for all he has given us. I take the words Dick says and place them inside my heart along with the hope that we will soon hear Donna speak again. She looks good, and she is eating better than she has in a long time. The gauntness has left her face, and when she smiles it is like the years have rolled back.

Beneath the tree sits a mountain of presents. Many of them are small things: a pair of socks, a box of notepaper, a bottle of nail polish. The joy of this night does not come from the value of the gift; it comes from the fun of being together, giving and getting small surprises.

Our baby sister, Geri, has gone overboard in being creative. She arrives with stockings filled with gifts for everyone, and this is the year of the walnut. There are two or three walnuts in every stocking. Some have been pulled open, the nutmeat scooped out, a small trinket placed inside, and then glued back together.

Donna, the practical joker in our family, is this night the butt of the walnut jokes. As we one by one pry open the walnuts, I shout, "Oh, wow, I got a key chain!"

Mama shouts, "Mine has a dollar bill inside!"

As Donna pries open her walnut and shows it to us, she mouths the words, *My walnut is just a walnut.*

We laugh. Then we move to the next round and the next. It is always the same; Donna's walnut is nothing more than a walnut. We all understand that this way of joking with Donna is our way of making her feel normal, of making her feel we have no need to tiptoe around her silence.

Donna can't speak and Floyd can't hear, but we are together. We are a family, and we are happy.

THIS WINTER MOVES FASTER than the one last year. It is broken up with moments of laughter and happiness as Donna prepares for her new grandchild.

She has little money to spend because her only income is what she receives from Social Security. We all offer to help out but she flatly refuses, so we do it in other ways. Mama takes the electric bill from her mailbox and pays it without Donna ever seeing it. I slide bills into her wallet and say nothing. Geri comes with boxes of groceries, and Debi tells her mom there was no co-pay on the medication.

We find ways to do these things, but we never act as if we are sorry for Donna. It is not something we speak of, but we all know being the object of pity is far worse than being sick or being poor. Being sick robs a person of their health and being poor robs them of life's luxuries, but being pitied robs them of their will to live.

IN EARLY MARCH DEBI'S friends plan a baby shower. By then Donna has scrimped and saved enough to outfit the crib. She has bought yellow and green print sheets, bumper pads, and pillows. Plus she has crocheted enough blankets to keep the child warm into adulthood.

You might think in a situation like this there is little to make a person unhappy, but some people are born unhappy and throughout their life they carry the need to share that unhappiness with others. Jim's mother is just such a woman.

Shortly after I'd receive an invitation to the shower, Debi calls me in tears. Under normal conditions she wouldn't know about the shower in advance, but this isn't a normal situation.

"Jim's mother told Ellen not to invite Mom because she's an embarrassment," Debi wails.

"What are you talking about?" I ask.

"The shower. Ann told Ellen not to invite Mom!"

"That's crazy," I say. "Why would she—"

"Because Mom has the tracheostomy and can't talk." Debi sobs. Then she says she's not going to the shower unless her mom comes.

"Did you tell Ellen that?" I ask.

"Of course I did."

"And what did Ellen say?"

"She's inviting Mom."

I breathe a sigh of relief. "Well, then…"

"But don't you see how awful—"

"Yes, I do see," I say sadly. "Ann should be ashamed of herself to even think such a thing."

"She's a mean person!"

"Yes, she is. But don't let one mean person ruin your special day." I'm seething, but I remain calm and logical for Debi's sake. "And don't ever tell your mom about this."

"I'd never tell Mom!" Debi screeches. "It would kill her!"

Before the thought has settled in my ear, I heave a weighted sigh. "It probably would."

We talk for a long time—an hour, maybe longer—but when we finally say goodbye Debi has come to terms with the situation. My hands tremble as I hang up the receiver. A cruelty to someone you love is far worse than a cruelty suffered yourself. The truth is I feel the same rage Debi feels, but I have nowhere to go with it.

The problem is gone. I tell myself to let it rest. Ellen has invited Donna, and the only people who know about Ann's words are Ellen, Debi, and me. It will remain with us. Donna will never know. I am determined that on the day of the shower I will surround my sister with an impenetrable wall of love.

Seating Arrangement

On the second Friday of March, Donna and Mama drive up to New Jersey. It is the day before the shower.

I am nervous at the thought of them driving such a distance alone, but no one has a say in what Donna does so all I can do is wait for their arrival. Several times I go onto the deck and scan the thin line of traffic crawling along Hillcrest Road, but not a single car turns off. Not one. Finally I take my book and sit on the deck where I can look across and see the road.

Fifteen minutes pass, and I am still on the same page. I read a sentence, look down the road, then back to the book. Having forgotten at what point I stopped, I return to the top of the page and start again. At long last I see the maroon Chrysler turn the corner, inching its way toward our house. A whoosh of relief comes up from my stomach.

Donna eases the car down the steep driveway, pulls to the far side, then switches off the ignition. She does not get out of the car.

I hurry down the stairs and rush to greet them. "I was so worried," I say, yanking the passenger side door open to help Mom from the car.

My sister leans across the seat and wriggles her fingers in a sign language hello. Jason sits between her legs like a co-pilot. Although she smiles and shakes off my question about being tired, I see a new weariness beneath her eyes. In the back seat of the car the big missile-shaped oxygen tank is wedged between several cartons of medical supplies.

I pretend not to notice this is practically a rolling hospital and act normal. Even though there is a knot of worry lodged in the center of my chest, I slide my arm around Donna's shoulder and tell her she looks good.

In some ways I am as helpless as her. I am her big sister. I want to make it better; I want to do something. Anything. I don't, because I love her too much. Saying "Lean on me, let me carry you and shoulder your burdens" would make me feel better, but it's not about me. I remind myself that loving my sister means I have to step back and give her the dignity of independence.

Donna has the car loaded with packages for the new baby. She has even crocheted pillow covers to match the array of granny square blankets. Her face is thin and gaunt, but it has a glow almost impossible to describe. She doesn't say anything, but she doesn't have to; her happiness is obvious.

After dinner Mama and Donna are both tired and go to bed early. "It's been a long day," Mama says.

As Donna walks toward the bedroom she claps her hands. Jason scoots from beneath the table and follows along.

Once they are beyond hearing range, I turn to Dick and say, "Donna doesn't look good, does she?"

He shrugs. "Actually, I think she looks better than last winter."

"That's just because she's happy about the baby."

"It's possible." He nods and returns to the newspaper he's reading.

I settle back into my thoughts knowing it's true. Just as worry can make a healthy person appear sickly, happiness can spread its glow across the face of the sick and make them appear more alive. This, I know, is the case with Donna. I see the rosy look of happiness on her face, but her hands are bone-thin and shaky. The telltale truth can be found in her hands.

ALTHOUGH MAMA HERSELF IS an early riser, she has raised three night owls. Neither I nor either of my sisters are early birds, but when I wake and stumble into the kitchen for my first cup of coffee Donna sits at the table dressed and ready to go.

"What's this?" I say jokingly.

She shrugs and gives me a sheepish grin. She mouths the word, *Anxious.*

I laugh. "We don't have to leave for another three hours." I pour my coffee and sit cross from her.

It's funny how I remember that one-sided conversation so vividly. My sister and I have a lifetime of shared secrets, most of them long forgotten, but not this one. In this strange combination of sign language and lip reading that we now have, she tells me of her experience with motherhood. Donna doesn't bother with the small words; she mouths only the words that carry weight. *First time. Holding baby. World changes.* The words are accompanied by actions of holding an invisible baby in her arms and the wide extension of her hands meaning "world."

Eventually words become too much for her. She pulls a napkin from the holder on the table and writes *I never thought I'd live to see my grandchild.*

A short while later when Mama walks in, Donna and I both have a stream of tears rolling down our cheeks.

"Who said what to whom?" Mama asks, and we all laugh.

LIKE EVERYONE ELSE, DONNA, Mama and I arrive at the shower well before Debi is scheduled to make an appearance. Unlike everyone else, when a whisper runs through the room saying the mother-to-be is about to walk in, we don't join the throng at the front of the room waiting to shout "Surprise!" Ann, of course, stands front and center.

We linger in the back and wait. Ellen and I are the only ones who know Debi is aware of what's happening.

As is the case at all showers, be it bridal or baby, the guest of honor gives a gasp of surprise. "Oh my gosh," Debi exclaims, "I had no idea!"

But even as she feigns her astonishment, I see her eyes scanning the room. When she asks, "Is my mom here?" Donna raises her hand and waves from the back.

Brushing past Ann with little more than a nod, Debi makes her way through the crowd and hurries back to Donna.

"Mom!" she squeals. "It's so good to see you!" Debi turns to the crowd. "Hey, everyone! This is my mom!" She gives Donna a smile, then turns back to the crowd. "She's not just my mom, she's the best mom in the world."

A tear rolls down Donna's face.

I told you Donna never cries, but that's not really true. She never cries about the disappointments and hurts most people would cry over, but she's softhearted when it comes to sentimentality. When a spark of emotion touches her heart, Donna is easily enough brought to tears.

After the food is eaten and the cake devoured, we

gather to watch Debi open the stacks of gifts mounded beside a chair decorated with ribbons. Ann sits in the chair next to it.

Debi sits, then turns to Ann. "Would you mind scooting over so my *mom* can sit next to me?" She says this in a pleasant voice, but she leaves no doubt that it is to be done. Before Ann's butt is out of the chair, Debi waves Donna over.

I know all aunties love their nieces, but my love for Debi is different, bigger, and more powerful. It's the kind of love you'd have for your own child. Or your sister. I have to love her this way, because she is a younger version of Donna. This day she is not thinking of being the star of the show; she is more concerned with being Donna's voice. I glow with pride.

As Debi unwraps gifts she passes them to Donna who wordlessly holds up each item for the crowd to see. She doesn't have to speak; Debi speaks for her.

"Oh," Debi says, "this adorable sweater set is from Aunt Geri…"

Although Donna's meager income is barely enough to cover expenses, she has somehow gathered a stack of gifts for the baby. The crocheted items are handmade, but the others she bought. I would gladly replace the money she spent for these gifts, but I don't. To do so would take away the joy of sacrifice. To give a lot when you have a lot is easy; but to give a lot when you have so little is indeed a gift of love.

When the day ends, Donna is weary but happy. She has shared in Debi's joy without ever knowing of Ann's comments.

TALK TO ME, BABY

In April the baby is born. It is a boy, and Debi names him Anthony. Once Debi is home from the hospital Donna drives up for a visit. I watch her holding the baby and see the love in her face. It is a strange look, mostly happy but with sad undertones that aren't visible unless you study her eyes.

As she holds the baby, Donna makes sounds. Nothing understandable, more like a sigh that has somehow forced its way through her useless larynx. In her face there is a restlessness that has been missing for the same amount of time as her voice.

TWO MONTHS AFTER DONNA holds her grandson, I get a call from Mama.

"Can you come down? Donna is having the tracheostomy reversed, and I need you to go to the hospital with me." Mama sounds annoyed.

"Isn't this good news?"

"Depends on your point of view," Mama comments. She doesn't have to say this thought is stuck in her craw; the tone of her voice says it for her.

"What does Doctor Craig say?"

"He says it can be done, but he'd rather she wait until her emphysema is more controlled."

When Mama is not in favor of something she loathes to talk about it, so I have to pull the bits and pieces of information from her.

"Why is Donna going against his advice?" I ask.

"Because she's Donna! She never listens to anybody! She's damned and determined to do what she wants and doesn't care about driving me to my grave with worry."

Now the truth is out. Mama doesn't want Donna to have the operation because she's afraid of losing her. Mama doesn't go at problems head on anymore; she circles the issue and spears it with cryptic barbs.

"Don't worry," I say, "I'm sure Donna knows what she's doing. Doctor Craig wouldn't—"

"What do you know? You're up there in New Jersey! You don't see how bad she is."

"I saw her when she was at Debi's, and I saw her again last month—"

"That's what you're going by?" Mama asks cynically. "You can't go by that! She puts on an act when she's up there."

"An act?"

"Yes, an act. She pretends she's fine, but she's not! She hardly eats a bite and sits in that damned recliner from dawn 'til dark."

"Well, I know her energy level is low, but that's to be—"

"That's not even half of it!"

I know this discussion is not going anywhere, so I say, "Maybe we can talk about it when I come down."

"It'll be too late by then, the surgery's scheduled for day after tomorrow."

"I'll come down tomorrow."

"Well, okay, but get started early."

OF COURSE, NOTHING MAMA or I had to say could convince Donna not to go through with the surgery. On her notepad she wrote, *I want this tracheostomy reversed.* That was the end of the discussion.

When you're up against a person who hasn't been able to speak for almost two years, any argument you make sounds lame by comparison.

TWO MONTHS AFTER ANTHONY'S birth, Mama and I once again sit in the waiting room at Johns Hopkins Hospital. They have redecorated the room, and now the walls are a pale yellow. The pumpkin seats that were there last time have been replaced by alternating blue and green molded plastic shells. These colors are supposed to be cool and relaxing, but I miss the pumpkin chairs. At least they had a thin layer of padding in the seat.

The center of the room is no longer an expanse of emptiness. It has been filled with two additional rows of blue and green shells. Why, I can't say. Every time we've been here the room is near empty, occupied by only a few unhappy souls who twitch and turn as we do, worrying about a loved one.

Today there is a young boy, a mirror image of the man sitting beside him. Father and son, I think. I find myself hoping they are waiting for another child to come into the world. Yes, that would be something nice; another child, instead of heart failure, cancer, or the dreaded emphysema. The boy shuffles through a handful of books, selects the one with a blue whale on the cover, and passes it to his father. He climbs onto the waiting knee and the man begins to read in a slow toneless drone; eventually his words grow dim to my ear and are lost in the sounds of crackling loudspeakers and footsteps clicking along the marble corridor.

We wait, but time weighs heavily upon us. I want to believe miracles are possible, but I question how the tracheostomy can be reversed when Donna still suctions out huge amounts of ugly green phlegm. I am caught between my fear of the consequences and the desire to hear my sister's voice again, so I turn away and try to ignore the truth.

Mama has found a matchbook sewing kit in her purse, and she is repairing the small hole that has fingered its way into her jacket pocket. She concentrates on this, weaving her needle back and forth, creating a fabric where there was none. It is something that enables her to escape the here and now.

I flip through several magazines and twist uncomfortably in the plastic shell. Eventually I get up and go to the window in an effort to escape the sadness of this room. The parking lot still stretches across the horizon, but each time the view is different. I have peered from this window when the hot summer sun bubbled the blacktop, when the spring rain slicked the ground with sheets of water, and when drivers had to scrape ice from their windshield before they drove away. Today the air is chilly, but the trees still look festive in their dress of bright orange and yellow. The colors remind me of the pumpkin chairs, and again I miss them.

Strange how you can miss something even though you weren't all that crazy about it in the first place. You don't miss it because it was special, only because it was familiar. The pumpkin chairs were here and they were familiar; now they're gone.

We have been here almost five hours when Doctor Craig comes into the room.

"You'll be able to see Donna in an hour or two," he says. "As soon as she is out of recovery."

I ask how the operation went.

"As well as could be expected."

This answer makes me nervous. I was hoping to hear something more positive. I wait a moment thinking there will be more, but when nothing else is said I ask, "Will she be able to speak?"

"Yes," he answers, "but she'll need oxygen."

"Why?" Mama asks.

Doctor Craig explains in lay terms that although they removed a considerable amount of scar tissue from Donna's trachea, her lungs are far from healed. He goes on to detail the procedure for closing the tracheostomy with a removable plug and indicates that it can be reopened if necessary.

"I would have preferred to leave it as it was," he says, "but Donna insisted on having the tracheostomy reversed."

"What's that mean?" Mama asks nervously. "That it will be harder for her to breathe?"

He pauses for a moment, fingers his brow, then answers, "Hopefully with medication and a steady supply of oxygen, she'll do okay."

I don't like the sound of his answer. Hopefully?

THE DAY AFTER THE operation Donna sits up watching television when we arrive at the hospital. A thick gauze pad is taped across the hole in her throat, and a clear plastic mask covers her nose and mouth. Through a mist of oxygen and moisture, we can see her lips curl into a smile at the sight of us.

Hesitantly, I say, "Hello," then wait.

In a coarse, gravelly voice, Donna crackles, "Hi."

It sounds nothing like the way she used to speak, but this is the first word she has said in two years. Mama and I both start talking at once.

"Thank God," Mom says, her eyes growing teary.

I lean across the bed and kiss my sister. The knobs poking out at her elbows and wrists have grown larger, and the bones of her chest are like those of a skeleton. I wonder if her appetite will come back now that she will be able to taste the flavor of the food again.

"Can you eat anything?" I ask.

"Just soft stuff for a few days," she crackles.

It is enough; I am encouraged and try to picture the plumpness returning to her arms and breasts.

Even though Donna is weary and speaks little we do not want this visit to end, so we stay until the nurse tells us to leave.

It is one of the only times I remember walking out of that hospital happy.

CHRISTMAS

Now that Donna is able to speak I am determined to make this the best Christmas ever. I spend almost a month on preparations and order a crown roast of pork so large it will barely fit in the oven. Knowing pork is Donna's favorite I add sausage stuffing in the center and hope she will pile on double helpings.

We have much to celebrate this year. Not only is Donna able to speak but Anthony is now eight months old, an age when the lights and sounds of Christmas create a magical world of wonder. Anthony is the first grandchild in our family, and we have bought him more toys than he can possibly play with.

I tell Dick, "This year we need a tree that's *really* special."

He cringes at the thought of what means, and he is right in doing so. Our search takes us to a tree farm in

Pennsylvania where we find *the tree*. It is too big to fit through the machine that secures the branches with plastic netting, so they wind it round and round with cord and then move it to the top of our car. Only then do I realize the true size of this tree; tied up, it is as wide as the car and almost twice as long.

This is the biggest tree we have ever had, almost fifteen feet high with wide reaching branches that sweep into the center of the room. Most of the rooms in our house are small, but the add-on family room is huge and has rafters crossing beneath a cathedral ceiling. This is where we set the tree. It is so tall the top branches spiral up between the rafters and scrape the slanted side of the ceiling.

"Perfect," I say.

From beneath a sweaty brow Dick smiles.

After we've wound a dozen strands of little white lights through the branches, we start to add ornaments. This is the most enjoyable part of tree trimming. There are hundreds of ornaments, some of which date back to my childhood. Like a pack rat I have carried them with me from place to place year after year. There is a story attached to almost every ornament.

"Debi made this when she was in kindergarten," I say, holding up a Styrofoam ball covered with a tattered piece of lace and dotted with sparkles. I tuck it into a high branch near the back.

Dick only half listens; he has heard these stories many times before. This doesn't stop me. I continue to tell the story of each ornament as I unwrap them one by one. After we have found an appropriate place for each one, even those that are old and dented and scarred, Dick climbs down from the ladder and we step back to admire this work of art.

"Beautiful," he says.

I respond with a sigh and say, "It's the best tree we've ever had."

I am expecting this to be the best Christmas ever. We have much to celebrate. The days ahead are like the presents. They glitter and promise much, but they are yet to be unwrapped. Just as others anticipate what is in the boxes, I anticipate what is yet to come.

MAMA, FLOYD, AND DONNA arrive on the evening of December twenty-third. I offer to make a late dinner, but they refuse.

"We ate on the way up," Mama says. "Floyd likes the Maryland-style crab cakes."

Donna says she'll have a drink, so I fix her a rye and Coca Cola and serve it with chunks of cheese and crackers. She is still painfully thin, and this disappoints me. I had hoped that once she no longer had the taste of metal in her throat she would begin to eat more. But apparently that hasn't happened.

She finishes that drink and then pours herself another. The cheese and crackers remain untouched.

ON CHRISTMAS EVE I get out of bed at the crack of dawn. There are still a few presents left to wrap, but first I polish the silver, set the table, peel potatoes, cut slices of celery, and chop onions for the stuffing as I sing along with the carolers on the stereo. I keep the music low in the hope of not waking our guests, but when I lift my head Mama stands in the kitchen doorway.

"What can I do to help?" she asks.

"Grab a cup of coffee," I say, nodding toward the Mister Coffee. "Then you can grate some carrots if you want."

She does as I ask and we sit across from each other at the kitchen table, sharing chores and conversation. This is the way Mama likes it to be.

By this evening a crowd will have gathered around the dining room table and before the night ends sounds of laughter and song will echo through the house, but for now it is just the two of us and the kkrrsh, kkrrsh of carrots sliding along the old handheld grater.

"You do have Miracle Whip?" Mama asks.

"Mayonnaise," I say.

"It's got to be Miracle Whip. Carrot salad needs Miracle Whip."

"Isn't mayonnaise the same thing?"

"Absolutely not," she says. "It has to be Miracle Whip."

Mama doesn't do a lot of cooking, and carrot salad is one of the few things she takes pride in doing.

Rather than disrupt the harmony of the moment I suggest, "I'll go to the store."

When I get to the supermarket there is not a parking space to be found. I circle the lot several times, then turn around and go home. In the garage I take an old boot and throw it into a brown paper bag. This is what I carry upstairs and clunk down on the side counter, acting as if I got the Miracle Whip.

"I'll finish up," I say. "You can take a shower before Donna needs the bathroom."

"Good idea." Mama nods.

Once she leaves the kitchen I add several spoons of mayonnaise to the grated carrots and move to the next chore.

A short while later Donna joins me in the kitchen. "Morning," she says in the gravelly voice that is foreign to my ear.

She is painfully thin. Her dry, colorless skin hangs loose over her bones like a garment on a wire hanger, yet she smiles as if nothing is wrong. I want to believe a smile means she is feeling better, so I tell myself it's just a matter of time.

"Would you like bacon and eggs?" I ask.

She frowns and shakes her head. "Just coffee."

I pour the coffee, add extra cream, and hand it to her, along with a plate of still-warm biscuits. She ignores the biscuits and takes a single sip of the coffee.

Although I have promised myself that I will make

this a festive holiday for her, I can no longer hold back the question troubling my mind.

"Have you seen the doctor lately?"

She turns away and looks absently out the window. "I don't want to talk about it."

"Maybe not, but –"

"No buts. I don't want to talk about it."

"I just thought –"

She doesn't raise another objection but gives me a look that indicates the conversation is over. Still determined to rebuild my sister, I pour a glass of orange juice and hand it to her. "Here, this is good for you."

She accepts it. I continue mixing fruit into the ambrosia, but I see her take the bottle of whiskey from the bottom cupboard and add a sizable measure to the juice.

"Do you really need that?" I ask, my annoyance obvious.

She nods. "I need something to get started this morning." She acts as if there is nothing unusual about drinking whiskey at ten o'clock in the morning.

When I give her a disapproving frown, she says, "Lighten up."

Before she has time to add anything else, I speak my mind.

"You're not eating enough, and you're drinking way too much!"

"I know what I'm doing," Donna answers angrily.

"No, you don't! You're killing yourself! Is that what you're trying to do? Kill yourself?"

For a moment she looks at me and says nothing. I have crossed the line that forbids us to speak of this possibility, and I am sorry. Were it possible to stuff the words back into my mouth and swallow them whole I would, but it is too late. All I can do is stand there in the naked glare of my mistake.

Donna takes a slow drink of the whiskey-laden juice then speaks. "You're wrong. I'm not trying to kill myself. I'm trying to enjoy the life I have left, and it's not easy."

"Don't talk like that," I say, but by then she's caught by a coughing spell and waves me off.

Although we leave the conversation there, the thought remains in my head.

AT THREE O'CLOCK THE rest of the family starts arriving. Donna spends most of the day in the recliner with Jason by her side and Anthony in her arms. She moves her hand back and forth in a slow gentle motion, first talking to Anthony then stroking the dog. She has enough love to satisfy both.

After the dinner dishes have been cleared away, I notice Donna no longer sits in the recliner. She has been gone for some time and I am concerned, so I go in search of her. It is easy to track her; I simply follow the plastic tubing that comes from the large oxygen tank.

The trail leads to the bathroom, but the plastic clip that should be in my sister's nose is outside the door.

I rap loudly on the door. "Donna, are you in there?"

"Yeah." The word is broken by a hacking cough before it is completed and sounds more like, "Yearrkkk, arrkkk."

"Are you okay?" I rattle the knob, but the door is locked. "Let me in."

"No, I'm on the john." She gives another hard cough then says, "Go away. I'll be back in a minute."

"You need help?"

This time her answer sounds impatient. "No. Go away."

I turn to walk away, but at the end of the hall I stop. I want to make certain she is all right. When the door finally clicks open, I slip around the corner so Donna won't know I have been watching and waiting. She walks slowly and holds to the furniture as she moves. The oxygen clip is back in her nose.

The line between being helpful and suffocating someone with unwanted care is a fine one and easy to cross when it's a person you love. I wait and give Donna time to make her way across the room. When she settles into the recliner I go to her and squat beside the chair. My intent is to ask if she needs anything, but before I get the chance I get a whiff of it.

It's the unmistakable odor of cigarette smoke.

Although such a thought seems incredulous, I lean close and whisper, "Have you been smoking?"

She turns her head and looks square into my face, dismissing the question with an indignant glare and a shake of her head. It is not convincing.

I leave her and return to the hall bathroom. The window is open and cold air is rushing in, but the odor of tobacco still lingers. Once you've been a smoker, you know the smell. Regardless of how long ago you gave it up, that odor is forever recognizable. It's like a song that brings the memory of a long-ago love.

There is no longer a question; I know Donna was smoking in here. Everyone else had been warned not to smoke inside the house.

"Donna is on oxygen," I explained. "A cigarette spark can cause an explosion."

That's why the oxygen clip was left in the hall.

Truth is an unrelenting thing. When it comes and slaps you in the face, you have no choice but to see it for what it is. *Why?* I ask myself. *Why?*

Inside I feel the rage of a thousand bulls. I want to scream and smack my sister's face until I shake some sense into her. But I do nothing, because it is Christmas Eve and she is happy with her children and new grandson. During the past two years there have been few times of such happiness, so I hold back my anger and say nothing. For now.

I pass the remainder of the evening doing as I have always done: handing out presents, passing around desserts, wishing those who depart a safe journey and finding those who stay clean sheets and a comfortable place to sleep. When the house is quiet and Dick and I are alone in our room, I tell him what I have discovered. He listens with his eyes riveted to my face as I speak.

"I don't know what to do," I say.

"What can you do?" he answers. "I know you love your sister, but she's the one who's in charge of her life. You can't make these decisions for her."

Ignoring this logic, I say, "This could kill her."

"Maybe, but it's still her choice." As he folds his sweater and slips it into the drawer, he shakes his head sadly.

Far into the night I lie awake thinking about what I now know and wondering what to do. As the faint light of Christmas morning breaks across the sky, I vow not to ruin Donna's day. After the holiday is over, I will visit her alone and we can talk about this.

I close my eyes and pray that I'm wrong. Maybe the smell was only of drinks and sweat and printed gift-wrap. Perhaps my mind has focused too hard on a problem where none exists.

"Please, God," I pray, "let it be that I am wrong."

THE TRUTH

January is a mean month. It's cold, blustery, and eventless. Nothing good can come of January. Today it is too cold to snow, but dark gray clouds hang low across the horizon erasing any definition between the earth and sky. This is January, a colorless sky, remnants of leftover snow and leafless trees.

I am on my way to Baltimore. Alone. Donna is not expecting me, and when she hears what I have to say she most likely will wish I hadn't come.

After what seems to be a longer-than-ever drive, I pull into the parking lot in front of her apartment complex. I climb from the car, walk to the entrance, and ring the doorbell. She is slow in answering, so I stand and shuffle my feet to keep warm. After a long while the curtain parts, and she peeks out to see who is at the door. As the buzzer sounds, I hear her throaty voice say, "Sorry, I was in the bathroom."

Doing what? I wonder.

As soon as she opens the door I hug her and sniff her clothing. It is a musty smell, maybe smoke, maybe not. Right away I say, "I've got to use the toilet," and hurry down the hall.

There is only one bathroom in her apartment, and I need to see if it smells of tobacco. As the door clicks shut, I take a deep breath. I am looking for the scent of cigarettes, but there is none. I sniff the air again and again, but all I get is the fragrance of rose petals. It is an overly sweet scent that makes me suspicious, so I start to poke around.

First I check the medicine cabinet. Nothing but vials of prescription drugs, a thermometer, and a bottle of aspirin. Next I turn to the storage cabinet and riffle through boxes of saline solution, gauze pads, plastic hoses, and clamps of one kind or another, but there are no cigarettes. I am almost ready to admit my error when I remember the built-in hamper and pull down the door.

One by one I go through soiled pajamas, socks, and panties; then I find it. Halfway down there is a plastic bag that contains three packs of cigarettes. Two unopened, the third half-empty.

I remove the cigarettes from their hiding place and head for the living room. "What the hell is this?" I say, angrily waving the bag at her.

Donna doesn't even blink an eye. She adjusts the oxygen clip in her nose and pushes the footrest of her recliner into position.

"Well?"

She looks at me defiantly and says, "I'd call it cigarettes. What would you call it?"

This is the same girl who ran away from home and hitchhiked to Virginia because Mama wouldn't allow her to wear jeans to school. I am no threat. The truth is Donna answers only to Donna. You can love her or hate her, but you will never control her. I know this, and tears well in my eyes.

"How could you?"

"It isn't like there's a lot else I can do." She shrugs.

"Yes, there is. You could at least try to get well."

She narrows her eyes and gives me a look as hard-edged as a knife. "Don't you think I've tried?"

"You've got to keep trying." I try to sound positive, but my words sound thin and desperate. "You've got emphysema! You shouldn't even be in a room where somebody is smoking, never mind doing it yourself."

"You think you know everything, don't you?" Donna lowers the footrest and sits upright, looking me square in the face. It's almost as if she has zeroed in on the bridge of my nose the way a bomber pilot locks a target in his sights, but there is no contact because I blink and look away.

I cannot make myself look into her eyes, for I know the truth is there. She is still the sister I grew up with, the one who was tough and strong. Wonder Woman.

"Look at me," she commands.

"Let's not go there," I say. The sound of her voice

tells me she has a comeback, but I don't want to hear it. The only thing I want to hear is that she will let go of these poisonous nicotine sticks.

"Look at me," she repeats. "Look at my face, because you need to understand what I am saying."

Several silent minutes pass before I allow my eyes to meet hers. In that single moment the years fall away. There is no sickness; we are simply two sisters, and she is the stronger one. Although every part of her body has failed her, Donna's rebellious spirit and determination have grown stronger.

There is no flippancy in her voice, no smile on her face. "Did you ever see a fish in a dried-up stream?"

"That has nothing to do with…"

"Did you?"

I reluctantly shake my head.

"I have! When a stream dries up, the fish suffocate on air. Their body flip-flops around looking for one more puddle, any little wet spot that will keep them alive for a few minutes longer. It doesn't matter how muddy or contaminated that water is, it's their only hope. Those fish are as good as dead, but they keep trying to hang onto the little bit of life they're got left."

"Donna, don't –"

"For once in your life, Bette, shut up. It's important that you understand this."

Donna blinks back what could be the start of tears, then continues. "Even when the stream is dry as a bone the fish keep sucking in air. There are no more puddles, but the poor dumb fish don't know that so they prolong the suffering, hoping against hope that they'll find another puddle.

"Eventually their eyes bulge out of their heads, and they die. It's slow and it's painful."

"But, Donna…"

She holds up a bony hand to stop me. "I don't have a lot of time; Doctor Craig has already said that. And I'm not going to use whatever time I do have flopping around like a half-dead fish."

"It doesn't have to be that way," I plead. "Now that the tracheostomy has been reversed, you'll get better."

She gives me a cackle-like laugh. "You know that's not true."

"Doctor Craig would have—"

Again, she laughs. It's not a real laugh but more the sound of sarcasm pushed into what once was a laugh. "He reversed the tracheostomy because I insisted on it. He wanted to keep it in because he thought it in would prolong my life expectancy."

"Isn't that what you want?"

"No," she answers and gives me another corkscrew look of disdain. "Doctors don't say, 'You've got three months to live and then it's sayonara.' But I feel the different parts of my body shutting down. I'm dying piece by piece."

"You don't know that."

"Yes, I do," she says without batting an eye. "I don't want to live like this. It takes every ounce of energy I have just to breathe enough air to survive."

I move across the room and kneel beside her chair. I search for the right words but find none.

"My lungs have gotten progressively worse. Every test –"

Although I know this is a time when I should do nothing more than listen, I blurt out, "That's because you're smoking."

"No, it isn't," she answers patiently. "It's been this way for the past two years. Each scan shows more deterioration than the time before."

"That doesn't mean—"

"Yes, it does." She nods. "I'm going to die soon, and there are things I need to say and do before it happens."

I have no more words, so I sit and let tears fall while I listen.

Donna tells me she wants time to say goodbye to her family and let Mama know how much she's appreciated. "Mama's like a little kid who needs to be praised."

Despite the weight of this conversation I snicker, because what she says is true. When we play cards or board games we all let Mama win. Not all the time but often enough that she feels happy with herself.

"I understand why you'd want the tracheostomy closed," I say, "but why smoking and drinking?"

She laughs. It's a hollow sound, but in a strange way it is Donna. "Because I enjoy it."

I start to sob. "Maybe if—"

Donna wraps her bony arm around my shoulder. "Don't cry. We're running out of time, so let's not spend it being sad."

For a long while we sit without speaking. She is resigned to what lies ahead; I am still struggling with it.

Although the original plan was for me to return home the next morning, I stay with Donna and we cling to these moments that are still ours. We reminisce about the things we have done together and express sadness over things we will never get to do. I try not to cry, but at times it's impossible.

"Promise me," she says, "that you'll watch over the kids."

"Promise," I answer. The word is like shredded glass coming from my throat, thick with the reality of what is to come. Although I have walked beside her through these years of struggle, it is still unbelievable that I will one day turn and Donna will no longer be there.

For the first time in all our years, we talk of life and death.

"I'm not afraid of dying," Donna says, "but I'm afraid of leaving a hole where I once was."

"A hole?"

She nods. "An empty spot in everybody's life." She wheezes for air then continues. "Debi and Charlie won't have a mom to turn to. Mama won't have somebody to watch after her. And you—" Donna's voice cracks, and she goes back to breathing through the oxygen mask.

BY THE THIRD DAY we are both weary of the sadness, so Donna suggests we get out of the house and have some fun. She spreads liquid makeup across her face and adds a pink glow to her cheeks. With a bulky winter coat covering her body, she looks less frail.

"Better," I say and smile as though I mean it.

At the mall I rent a wheelchair, and we stroll the aisle browsing the window displays. Afterwards we go to lunch. At five-thirty we leave the mall and head for home.

It has been a long and tiring day, but Donna wants to say hello to her old friends.

"Let's stop at the Crab House," she says.

"Okay." I smile.

As we climb the three steps, she leans on my arm. Inside the bar is still dimly lit and the music loud, but everything else has changed. A pool table now sits in the center of what used to be the dance floor, and a female bartender in a black silk vest and red bow tie has replaced Harry. Most of the stools are empty, and to those who are at the bar Donna is a stranger.

"What's your pleasure?" the bartender asks.

Donna waves the girl off. "I was just looking for a friend," she says. Then she turns back to the door, and we leave.

As we drive away, I can see how the disappointment stoops her shoulders.

ON FRIDAY I DRIVE home with the hard truth of reality pressing against my chest. I want to be strong like Donna but I'm not, and so I cry all the way up the New Jersey turnpike.

A Sad Goodbye

For what will be the last time Mama and I take Donna to Johns Hopkins Hospital. We go directly to the emergency entrance, and she is admitted within the hour. We stay with her and follow along as they wheel her upstairs to a private room. Donna is pale, and her eyes have faded from hazel to the color of cold dishwater.

The nurses seem to know what is ahead, and long after the last visitor chime has sounded they pass us and say nothing about leaving. We have already called Geri and Donna's children. Tomorrow they will all be here. It is after ten when we start to leave. I lean over the bed to kiss my sister goodnight and I whisper, "Hang on, Donna."

She flickers her eyelids and gives a weak smile.

IT IS CLOSE TO MIDNIGHT when Geri arrives at Mama's house. Debi and Charlie come in fifteen minutes later. This time there are no spouses; it is just the five of us. Floyd has already gone to bed, and the others will come tomorrow. We talk and stay together long into the night.

When the sun has barely creased the horizon, we climb from our beds and start for the hospital, the five of us in one car. It is too early for visitors, and we know that, but we need to be there. We walk quietly through the lobby and ride the elevator to the third floor. No one stops us when we go into Donna's room.

She is sleeping, so we stand by the wall and wait.

When Donna opens her eyes a short while later, she sees Debi and stretches out her hand. Debi moves to the bed and takes the frail hand in hers.

We remain here throughout the day. Although only two visitors at a time are allowed, no one mentions that we are five and they allow us to stay and spend precious moments together. At eight o'clock that evening Janice, the nurse who has been with Donna for most of the day, comes in and urges us to leave.

"Patients need to get their rest," she says.

We leave and return to the house. Mama suggests, "I can order a pizza. Or a bucket of chicken."

"No, thanks," we say.

No one is hungry. No one is sleepy. We simply wait.

In the wee hours of the morning the telephone rings. We know before Mama answers what the caller will say, and we start to cry.

THREE DAYS LATER DONNA was laid to rest. I could tell you of the funeral, of the people who came, of the countless tears that were shed and the way Mama shrunk to a size that could slide through a keyhole, but the truth is if you've ever lost someone you love you know of all these things.

For weeks people came bearing gifts of food and flowers. They promised prayers and lit candles. They showered us with condolences and whispers of how she is now at peace. At the time it was hard to believe such a thing, but I have since come to see the truth in it.

Donna was too full of life to linger on death's doorstep. She wanted it to be over. She wanted to move on, and she wanted us to move on. I am certain that somewhere in this vast universe there's a party going on, and she's now part of it.

There were a number of things Donna was wrong about. She was wrong to think smoking was harmless. She was wrong to choose Charlie as a husband. She was wrong to think she could run away from home, and no one would care.

But she was right when she said she'd leave a hole. She did. A hole so large that I could live for a thousand years and still not be able to replace her.

Gone but not Forgotten

Two seasons passed before I could find heart enough to smile. From the window of my office I watched the snow disappear and buds spring to life on bare branches. The lilacs that stretch across our yard blossomed as fragrant and sweet as bubble bath, but I kept the windows shuttered. The smell of flowers was little more than a reminder of the time I tried to forget.

I held to the heartache of that bitter winter for many months. Long after the sun turned hot and the lawn grew thick, I felt cold and wore wooly slipper socks on my feet. I thought about Donna every day, but the good memories didn't come to mind. Instead I saw the picture of her gasping for breath and heard the sound of her pen tapping the telephone.

In August the dreams began.

At first I would wake with a start and although I could recall seeing my sister, I remembered nothing else. Little by little, the visitations became more detailed and in the morning I would linger on the edge of sleep trying to hold on to the dream for safekeeping in my memory.

In the beginning the dreams were like an eight-millimeter film with no sound: choppy little segments of our life spliced together. Mama was young, her hair dark and without strands of gray. Donna and I were kids. In some dreams we were eight and ten, and in others we were teenagers. We were always young and carefree. After a while the dreams broadened and became spirited conversations.

In the waning days of summer, a single dream came back time after time. It was a replay of the day Donna tried to teach me to ride a bike.

"YOU'RE NEVER GONNA GET this if you're afraid of falling," she says.

"I'm not afraid," I answer, but even in the dream I can feel beads of sweat rising on my forehead.

Donna flashes a devilish smile. "Don't gimme that crap."

When I try to protest I inevitably snap to, and that's the end of the discussion. I am awake and Donna is gone.

FOR TWO WEEKS I kept remembering that day, and now I regret not trying harder. Donna was right, I was afraid of falling. She wasn't afraid of dying, but I was petrified of falling.

The truth stares me in the face. I am a coward. And as long as I remain a coward, I will never live life to the fullest.

THEY SAY THAT PROVIDENCE plays a part in everyone's life, and I believe it. Two days after I have come to see myself as I am, I find myself standing in front of Mac's Bicycle Shop. In the window is a bright red retro model, a replica of the one Donna rode. For a few minutes I stand there looking at it. Then I make a decision. Five minutes later I am loading that big bicycle into the trunk of my car.

I WOULD LIKE TO SAY I am not the least bit afraid when I climb on the bike, but it would be a lie. Before my foot touches the pedal, I am already picturing what it will be like to walk with a cast on my leg.

Like Donna, Dick claims riding a bike is easy.

"I'll get you started," he says.

He holds the bike steady, and I climb on. I push

down on the pedals, and the bike starts moving. He's holding the back end of the bike and running alongside. I start pedaling faster and feel the wind rush by.

"Oh, wow," I say. Then I realize he's no longer behind me.

"Hey," I yell, "what am I supposed to do now?"

From a half-block behind me Dick hollers, "Keep pedaling!"

I do.

ONCE I LEARNED TO keep myself upright I tackled the more difficult maneuvers, like rounding corners, slowing to a stop, and waving to a neighbor. Day by day I grew bolder. In time I had a basket mounted across the handlebars, plunked Brandi in it, and circled the block three times. Pretty soon we were zipping around the entire neighborhood, houses disappearing behind us one by one, Brandi's ears flapping in the breeze, the warm sun on my back.

We were Dorothy and Toto pedaling across Kansas—no cyclone, no wicked witch, no need for ruby slippers. I had something far more magical. I had my sister's ability to rise above fear.

I STILL FIND MYSELF thinking about Donna at least once a day, but the hole in my heart is starting to heal. I realize my sister is not really gone. She never will be. There is a wisecracking, ever-laughing memory that lives on, not just in my heart, but inside of everyone who knew and loved her. It is this memory that gives us the courage to move forward. Not forget; just move forward.

A short while back we had a reunion in Atlantic City, just the four of us—Mama, Geri, Debi, and me. We tried to weave a patch across the hole in our midst. It was early September; the sun felt warm and the smell of the ocean thick in the air. We bought bags of salt-water taffy and walked along the boardwalk reminding each other about Donna as she really was and retelling the stories of her life. It was a time for remembering but not for sadness. We did as Donna would have wanted; we celebrated her life instead of mourning her death.

Geri brought a roll of quarters for each of us to play the slot machines. Mama was an all-or-nothing woman. Her quarters were gone in the time it took to pull that lever forty times. Me, I still had most of my quarters at the end of the three days. I'm not much of a gambler; I like safe, sure things. I pick stocks like General Electric or IBM, I never cross before the light turns green, and I bring my umbrella if there's more than a ten percent chance of showers.

This is the way it has always been, me the cautious, practical sister, Donna the carefree daredevil. Plenty of times I resented that and tried to pretend I was above it all. I looked down my nose at the outrageous things she did, but the truth is I was jealous. I always thought life was kind of unfair; it seemed like she got the best of everything. Now I realize, she didn't get the best of everything, she just made the best of everything she got.

To most of us, "Blueberry Hill" is nothing more than a song, but to Donna it was a place. A place where dreams come true, a place where you can catch a firefly, find a four-leaf clover, get over a broken romance, and forget your troubles. I may never find my Blueberry Hill, but Donna gave me enough courage to search for it.

A Note from the Author...

This story is a work of fiction, and it's not. It is a memoir of sorts. It is the story of the last few years I shared with my sister, Donna. Most of it is true to the best of my recollection, but time clouds memories—especially memories of the things we choose to forget.

During these years there were many other people in Donna's life: our sister, Geri, Donna's son Charlie, friends, neighbors, co-workers, and the husband she married twice. These people all played huge roles in Donna's life, but they are simply passersby in this story. This is my story. A story of sisters and the bond we shared.

Donna was an enigma. At times she lived life with wild abandon, but once her first child came she was ready to settle down. She loved Charlie, loved him so much she married him twice. She also divorced him twice. She had no choice. For that reason I think I also partly blame Charlie for the pathway Donna chose.

More than an accurate timeline, this is a collection of stories culled from memory. I chose not to include graphic descriptions of the horrors that come, but suffice it to say once seen it is something you never forget.

You may find spots where you argue with the story, where you say this wasn't right, or she shouldn't have done that. Unfortunately that's how life is. It doesn't always come wrapped in beautiful stories and tied with a bow.

Each day is a gift. Treasure it and remember it for what it is. There may come a time when that memory is all you have.

Award-winning novelist Bette Lee Crosby brings the wit and wisdom of her Southern mama to works of fiction—the result is a delightful blend of humor, mystery and romance. "Storytelling is in my blood", Crosby laughingly admits, "My mom was not a writer, but she was a captivating storyteller, so I find myself using bits and pieces of her voice in almost everything I write."

A *USA Today* bestselling author, Crosby has twenty-two published novels, including *Spare Change* and the Wyattsville series. She has been the recipient of the Reader's Favorite Gold Medal, Reviewer's Choice Award, FPA President's Book Award and International Book Award, among many others. Her 2016 novel, Baby Girl, was named Best Chick Lit of the Year by *Huffington Post*. Her 2018 novel *The Summer of New Beginnings*, published by Lake Union, took First Place in the Royal Palm Literary Award for Women's Fiction and was a runner-up for book of the year. Her 2019 release, *Emily, Gone* was a winner of the Benjamin Franklin Literary Award.

Crosby currently lives on the East Coast of Florida with her husband and a feisty Bichon Frise who is supposedly her muse.

To learn more about Bette Lee, visit her website at:
https://betteleecrosby.com